BILLY SURE

KID ENTREPRENEUR

IS A SPY!

INVENTED BY **LUKE SHARPE**
DRAWINGS BY **GRAHAM ROSS**

LIAR'S LEMONADE

Simon Spotlight

New York   London   Toronto   Sydney   New Delhi

SIMON SPOTLIGHT
An imprint of Simon & Schuster Children's Publishing Division
1230 Avenue of the Americas, New York, New York 10020
This Simon Spotlight edition March 2016
Copyright © 2016 by Simon & Schuster, Inc. Text by Michael Teitelbaum.
Illustrations by Graham Ross. All rights reserved, including the right of
reproduction in whole or in part in any form.
SIMON SPOTLIGHT and colophon are registered trademarks of
Simon & Schuster, Inc.
For information about special discounts for bulk purchases,
please contact Simon & Schuster Special Sales at 1-866-506-1949 or
business@simonandschuster.com.
Designed by Jay Colvin
The text of this book was set in Minya Nouvelle.
Manufactured in the United States of America 0216 OFF
10 9 8 7 6 5 4 3 2 1
ISBN 978-1-4814-5278-6 (hc)
ISBN 978-1-4814-5277-9 (pbk)
ISBN 978-1-4814-5279-3 (eBook)
Library of Congress Catalog Card Number 2015950428

Chapter One

Surprises

I'M BILLY SURE. UP UNTIL a MOMENT aGO, I THOUGHT I was a normal kid—a normal kid with normal schoolwork and a normal dog and normal chores. I've never felt anything but normal—okay, except for the fact that I'm also a world-famous inventor, but even then, still normal. Or so I thought.

But I just received the **FOUR BIGGEST SURPRISES OF MY LIFE**, each one bigger than the last. And now I'm not sure if I ever was normal.

Let me explain.

I'm thirteen years old. Actually, I turned

thirteen today. I'm also a seventh-grader at Fillmore Middle School, and I'm the world-famous inventor behind the company **SURE THINGS, INC.** I'm not saying that to brag or anything. I really don't like people who brag or who talk about how great they are. But to be honest, I am proud of what I have accomplished, even though my whole world just got thrown upside down!

Together with my best friend and business partner, Manny Reyes, I run Sure Things, Inc. Our company has invented a whole bunch of popular stuff, like the ALL BALL (a ball that can change into any kind of sports ball) and the CAT-DOG TRANSLATOR. Manny and I share an office. Well, it's really his parents' garage, but we've converted it into what the rest of the universe knows as the world head-quarters of Sure Things, Inc.

Anyway, a short while ago I arrived at the office after getting a panicked phone call from Manny. We had just finished judging a live TV special during which we picked Sure Things,

Inc.'s next product, or as we like to call it, the Next Big Thing.

On the TV special, we selected an invention called the NO-TROUBLE BUBBLE, a personal force field that can protect you from just about anything.

Two days after the show aired, Manny called me at home. He sounded super upset! He said that we had a problem with the No-Trouble Bubble that could result in the end of Sure Things, Inc.

Now that, as you can imagine, is pretty serious stuff. So I raced over to the office, hurried through the door, and, what do you know—I walked right SMACK! into a surprise party for my thirteenth birthday!

SURPRISE NUMBER ONE.

As it turns out, Manny's whole "we're in trouble" thing was a just ruse to get me over to the office, where my friends and family were waiting. My family being my dad, Bryan Sure, and Emily, my soon to be fifteen-year-old sister, who is, well . . . an older sister.

Usually my mom would be in that group too, but she's been away from home for a while. She works all over the world, and most of the time we have no idea where she is. She's a research scientist, or so she has always told me. In the weeks leading up to my big birthday (after all, you only become a teenager once), I had practically begged her to visit, but Mom kept saying that she couldn't make it.

Except she *could* make it. When Manny opened another door, I found out that Mom was: SURPRISE NUMBER TWO!

But then, a few minutes after Mom's unexpected appearance, she asked me to step away from the party and go outside with her so we could talk about something "in private."

Naturally, my mind started racing. What could she want to talk about that is so important and so secret?

My mom revealed SURPRISE NUMBER THREE. She's not really a research scientist. And nope, she hasn't been away in Antarctica like we thought. What I found out is something even cooler. My mom is a spy!

And then, immediately after, I received the FOURTH and by far THE BIGGEST SURPRISE OF ALL when Mom said to me:

"When I leave, I want you to come with me. I need your help."

So now? Now I'm stunned. I hardly know what to say. I stare at my mom in disbelief. Am I on the TV show *Prank Attack*, the one where they prank celebrities? I look closely at Mom's clothing. I peek around the backyard. No hidden camera or microphone. No one is jumping out of the bushes.

This is real!

I'll be honest. Manny and I have thought

my mom might be a spy for a while now. We've joked about it—especially a few months ago, after Mom sent me a "self-destructing" computer program to catch Alistair Swiped, a thief who was stealing my invention ideas. But then I remembered that Mom is just my mom. She's the kind of mom who orders in pizza and on more than one occasion laughed so hard that she spit all over my dad's shirt. The mom whose nickname for our dog, Philo, is O-MY-O PHILO! Could that same Mom really be a spy?

"I know it's a lot to absorb, honey," Mom says. She looks around, as if she is half-expecting a team of top secret ninja spies to leap from the bushes and arrest her just for having this conversation with me. "You can ask me any questions you want."

My mind is reeling. A thousand questions pop into my head, but I ask the most straight-forward one first.

"Who do you work for? The CIA? The FBI? The Secret Service?"

"I can't say," Mom says.

"You can tell me," I press.

"No, I really can't say," Mom replies. "I'm not trying to dodge your question, Billy, but if I tried to say the agency's name, my tongue would fall out." Then she looks kinda sad. "Poor Agent Lugman found out the hard way."

Gurg, gawk, blech, bluck, grack!

Is she for real?

"I'm thirteen," I say, coming to a realization. "That means you've been keeping this secret for thirteen years! Why tell me the truth now?"

"I am truly sorry, honey," she says, taking my hand. "It was just safer for the whole family if you and Emily didn't know. As to why now, well . . . I need your help. Specifically, your genius for inventing."

Mom sure knows my soft spot. Mention inventing and I'm all ears.

She continues. "Sometimes, we spies find ourselves in situations where our spy gear can be easily taken. Physical objects—even hidden ones like microphones in lipstick containers, transmitters in soda cans, lasers inside pens— can be found and confiscated by enemy agents.

"I wouldn't come to you, Billy, if we had another choice. But our agency's best inventors can't crack this code, and I think you can. We need an invention that is undetectable to enemy agents. We would like you to invent SPY DYE—a hair dye that combines all the functions of a spy's usual secret gear. Spy Dye should allow the agent to read minds, keep tech concealed, act as a personal force field, and do anything else you can cram into liquid form that can be worked into someone's hair."

Spy Dye—I smile to myself. Manny would definitely approve of that name. But thinking of Manny makes me think of other people too. How many people know Mom is a spy?

"Does Dad know about your real job?" I ask. My dad is notoriously bad at keeping secrets.

"Of course," Mom replies. "In fact, he helps me."

WHAT?! I'm not ready for SURPRISE NUMBER FIVE. My dad is a great guy. He's a painter, a gardener, and a cook (kind of). But a spy? That, most definitely, does not compute.

"You know some of those wacky meals he creates?" Mom continues.

"All too well," I reply. That's why I said Dad is *kind of* a cook, because he loves to do it but he's terrible at it! Fortunately, Sure Things, Inc. invented the GROSS-TO-GOOD POWDER not too long ago. Sprinkle a little bit on your meal and it makes anything, even Dad's cooking, taste great.

"It just so happens that some of those meals are actually coded messages from me," Mom says. "There are times when I can't afford to have someone discover my location or know where I'm headed from an e-mail. So your dad and I developed a code. Whenever I send him an e-mail suggesting that he make waffles, he knows that my case is solved!"

"That's pretty cool," I say. "Thanks for making your code waffles and not canned tuna fish."

Mom laughs.

"And depending on the type of ingredients I suggest, he knows when I'll be arriving at my next destination."

"So those pickle and pineapple waffles Dad made last week were actually a coded message?" I ask.

"Yes. That particular combination meant that my latest case was solved and I'd be coming home soon. That's how he knew that I'd be here for your party."

"What's the significance of waffles?" I ask, wondering if I would be good at breaking codes.

Mom shrugs. "Your dad likes waffles."

She takes a deep breath and looks at me. Really looks at me—the way she did when she dropped me off at school for the first time, and when she watches me slurp my cereal for breakfast, and when I sort the purple jelly beans from the pack.

"Billy, you've proven time and again that you can make even the wildest inventions happen. I'm afraid you are our last hope. Will you come with me to the agency's Spy Academy?"

As someone who has to deal with school, homework, running a business, being president of a club (the Fillmore Middle School Inventors Club), taking care of Philo, and dealing with an older sister (practically a full-time job by itself), I am used to juggling lots of things in my head. But the sheer enormity of all I have just learned, especially Mom's request, is kind of overwhelming.

But through the shock, surprise, worry, and confusion, one thought bubbles up to the front of my brain.

THIS IS THE COOLEST THING EVER!

I mean, I'm being hired by the government to create an invention . . . and one I don't even have to dream up from absolute scratch.

This Spy Dye idea is really intriguing, like a mash-up of lots of my previous work, but in liquid form. Plus, I'll get to spend time with my mom, something I hardly ever get to do.

So the answer, I think, is obvious.

"Like my name . . . SURE. I'll totally go with you to Spy Academy!" I say, thrilled beyond belief.

Mom gives me a big hug. "Thank you, Billy," she says.

"I can't wait to tell Manny and Emily and—"

Mom cuts me off right there.

"I'm sorry, Billy," she says. "This is top secret. You can't tell *anyone!* Not Manny, not Emily, not even Philo—not when you have a spare Cat-Dog Translator in your room!"

Chapter Two

The Cover Story

THE EXCITEMENT INSTANTLY DRAINS FROM MY body. I feel terrible having to keep a secret from Manny.

At that moment, Manny sticks his head out the door.

"Hey, Billy, I know you haven't seen your mom in a long time, but there other people here who want to wish you a happy birthday," he says, smiling.

"We'll be right in," I say.

Manny nods and then disappears back into the garage.

"I feel really bad having to lie to him," I admit.

"Don't worry, honey," Mom says, squeezing my shoulders, "I'll handle it. You won't actually have to tell Manny a lie."

Why does that not make me feel any better?

Mom and I head back into the party. Honestly, it's hard for me to focus on the good wishes and tasty treats. All I can think about is Spy Academy. It just doesn't seem real.

"Hey, everybody," Manny announces. "Let's all head outside. There's one more surprise—a big finale, if you will."

I follow Manny to SURPRISE NUMBER SIX in his backyard. A glow appears and starts moving toward me. By the flickering light I see that Emily is carrying a cake. As she gets closer, I realize that the cake is in the shape of an All Ball, the invention that got Sure Things, Inc. started.

She places it in front of me, and Manny hands me a small remote device.

"What's this?" I whisper.

"Just press the button," he replies.

Click.

Immediately after, there's a popping sound. **POP! POP! POP!** The candle flames jump out from the cake and create a mini fireworks display! It looks just as professional as any fireworks show I've ever seen. It's the coolest thing! At the end of the explosions, the lights float into the air like confetti and spell out *Happy Birthday, Billy!* before flickering off into the distance. Then everyone chimes in with a delightfully off-key version of the happy birthday song.

As Emily cuts the cake, I lean over to Manny.

"Looks like you've been busy doing some inventing on the side," I say, handing him back the remote.

"Oh, just a little something Emily and I cooked up as part of the surprise," he replies.

"You two make a good team," I say, but I feel a little guilty knowing that Emily is going to have to step in and help Manny with Sure Things, Inc. when I'm at Spy Academy.

Despite my guilt (and my jitters!), the rest of the party is really fun. Clayton Harris, one of the members of my inventors club, laughs so hard that chocolate milk comes out of his nose. And Petula Brown from my English class asks Manny to dance! (Manny's face turns BRIGHT RED like a giant strawberry. He then shuffles across the makeshift dance floor—which is really just a tarp from my workbench, stretched over the grass in Manny's backyard—and they dance to Dustin Peeler's new slow song.)

As the party starts to wind down, Mom pulls Manny and Emily aside. I stand next to her.

"Thank you so much for putting this party together," Mom says. "You two are awesome."

Manny and Emily beam.

"But I have to say, this party makes me feel bad," she continues. "I wish I didn't have to be away from home so much. So I was thinking about it . . . and I'm giving Billy a special birthday present. I'm taking him on a two-week trip to Barbados."

Manny and Emily both looked stunned. No surprise there.

"In the middle of the school year?" Manny asks. "Right when we have to roll out the No-Trouble Bubble—our Next Big Thing?"

"Uh, yeah," Emily chimes in. "What he said. But more importantly, why does Billy get to go to Barbados and not me?"

"Emily, for your birthday in a few weeks,

you'll get to go on a trip too," Mom says. "How does that sound?"

Emily sighs loudly. Knowing Emily, she will probably beg Mom for a trip to England to meet her favorite British celebrities. Emily loves British celebrities. She even pretended to have a British accent for a while.

In the middle of this conversation, I notice that each of Emily's nails is a different color. It didn't seem to be that way yesterday. I'm guessing this is her new "thing." Emily always has a new thing. Last week it was a chunky ring on every one of her ten fingers. It made it very hard for her to hold things.

"I've already spoken to the school and arranged for Billy to miss classes for the next two weeks. He'll have to make up the work, of course, but I think that this trip will be so good for him, and for us." She says "us" like she means all of us, and I remember that I'm supposed to invent Spy Dye to help the agency—and my country. That makes me feel really cool!

"But what about the No-Trouble Bubble and

Sure Things, Inc.?" Manny asks. Ever since we came out with the All Ball, I've hardly missed a day of work—and now I'm going to be out for two weeks!

Finally, I speak up. "Emily, I was kinda thinking that you could help Manny out with the company. After all, you are a Sure."

Emily rolls her eyes in the most dramatic way possible. She glares at me, her multi-colored fingernails on her hips, and then she lets out a deep sigh, as if I just asked her to count every grain of sand on every beach in the world. After filling her sulky girl quota, she smiles.

"Fine! I'll do it."

· · ·

The next few days are stressful. Mom and I are leaving for Spy Academy first thing Sunday morning, and I have to pack! What in the world does one bring to Spy Academy?

I pull out a big duffel bag from the back of my closet. The last time I used this was four years ago, when I went to CAMP LOTS O' ACTIVITIES. I shake some dirt and pebbles out of the bag, and they scatter all over my floor. *Self-cleaning floors*, I think to myself. *Not super exciting, but I bet adults would like that invention.*

And then I feel a little sad. Because what if it isn't just two weeks? What if I like Spy Academy? What if I stay forever?

What will happen to Sure Things, Inc.?

I open every drawer in my dresser and stare at my clothes. How many pairs of socks does someone at Spy Academy need? Will there be uniforms? Do I need special secret-agent sunglasses?

Usually, when I'm stuck like this, I talk

to Manny and he makes me feel better. But as Mom said, talking to Manny about Spy Academy is out of the question. So I decide to do something else instead that will make me feel better. I invite Manny over for a sleepover. I might not be able to talk about what's really going on, but at least I can have fun with my best friend before I go away!

Sleepovers are something we did a lot when we were little kids, but haven't for a while. I guess we've both just been busy.

"I have to say, Billy, I'm kinda nervous about working with Emily for such a long period of time without you around," Manny confesses as we gobble down homemade ice-cream sundaes that evening. "You know how bossy she can be."

"I do," I reply through a mouthful of whipped cream, nuts, cherries, and peanut butter chunks. "But she's way bossier with me. One of the PERKS of being family, I guess. You guys will be okay. And I really do appreciate this chance to spend some time with my mom."

21

"Well, as your friend I'm really happy for you," Manny says, wiping a long dribble of chocolate sauce from his chin. "But as your business partner . . ."

There's no need for him to finish that sentence.

That night we settle into sleeping bags on the floor of my bedroom. I guess I could sleep on my bed, but that sorta defeats the point of a sleepover.

I drift into a wild dream. In it, I'm wearing a trench coat, a fedora, and dark glasses. I hurry down a dimly lit alley, glancing back over my shoulder every few steps. When I turn back around, I am face to face with two nasty-looking goons!

"Well, well, well, who do we have here?" snarls one of the goons.

"My name is Sure. Billy Sure. I eat punks like you for breakfast!" I growl.

"We'll just see about that!" shouts the second goon, pounding his fist into the palm of his other hand. "If you'll just give us the secret defense codes, no one gets hurt."

"Go fly a kite, punks," I say, tipping the brim of my hat down over my forehead. "Preferably very close to a cliff."

They both rush toward me!

BUZZ! BUZZ! BUZZ!

At that second my alarm jolts me awake. It was all a dream! PHEW!

"Early flight, huh?" asks Manny as he rubs his eyes and rolls up his sleeping bag. "Have lots of fun! Send me a postcard. And watch out for sunburn."

For some reason, Manny doesn't look at me. Maybe he's really sad.

"Don't worry, Manny," I reassure him. "The time is going to just fly by. I'll be back before you know it."

If I come back, I think guiltily.

Chapter Three

Journey to Spy Academy

AFTER MANNY LEAVES, IT'S TIME TO GO. MOM LEADS me outside to a black unmarked car.

"Just in case anyone follows us," Mom says, and she opens the door for me. That's when I notice something really cool. Like, beyond cool. Like, cooler than ice cubes in lemonade cool.

The car—which from the outside is just a regular car—is GIANT on the inside. The seats look like long, sleek benches, and there are other cool things, like a dressing room, an archery practice field, and . . . an octopus?

"Don't mind Paul," Mom says. "Well, Agent Paul to you. He's my partner on secret missions, where he often lends me a hand—or eight!" She laughs at her own joke. I'm not sure, but it looks like Paul cracks a smile as well.

An octopus that's a secret agent? A car that expands when you get in it?

I'm sure your mom is cool, but my mom is definitely the coolest.

We drive across town. That's when I realize something.

"You're awfully quiet," says Mom as familiar streets and highways give way to new scenery.

"I'm a little nervous," I explain. "I mean, I'm okay with the inventing part. I just don't know who or what I'm going to meet when we get there. I mean, after all the success and hoopla of Sure Things, Inc., I am kinda used to publicity and being in the spotlight and meeting lots of new people. Still, I'd be lying if I said I don't get a little nervous in new situations."

"Everybody does, honey," Mom says, and I feel a little reassured. "Anyway, your days will be split between taking classes and working in the lab."

"Not so different from my days now," I say, starting to feel a little less nervous. "But why will I be taking classes? Aren't I there to invent Spy Dye?"

"You are," Mom says, but then her eyes get really narrow. "But there might be an opportunity for . . . later work. It's better if you get a little spy training just in case."

Later work? Spy training? That's pretty awesome, but what about Manny, *my* partner?

After more driving, Mom pulls into an old strip mall. It looks kinda like a scene from a horror movie, and part of me thinks a zombie is going to jump out from behind the Dumpster. More than half the stores are closed and shuttered. The only places open are a package-shipping store, a tiny thrift store, and, right in front of the car, a downright scary-looking diner with food that's probably worse than Dad's!

"Why are we stopping here?" I ask. "You don't want to eat at that place, do you?"

Mom smiles and shakes her head. "Just follow me."

She parks and grabs Agent Paul's tank. We get out, and I follow her into the thrift store, wondering exactly what is going on and why an octopus needs to join us. I know that my mom can be an impulsive shopper. I remember family car trips when I was little in which she would yell out, "Turn in there, Bryan, I just have to see that moldy old grandfather clock in the window!" Unless all this time she was doing secret spy stuff I didn't know about!

The inside of the store smells like a mix of cat litter and bananas. Practically every square foot of space is covered with shelves, old furniture, and stacks of weird books. One of the books is called *Dogs Are Aliens from Space and This Is Why!* Another is called *The Internet: What You Need to Know about the World's Newest Thing.* How old is this place?!

As I walk down the aisles, I see shelves jam-packed with cracked plates, bowls, drinking glasses, and tiny knickknacks that I think are older than my grandmother. Racks of used clothing are strewn about, and the walls are covered with crookedly hung pictures of sad clowns, dogs playing cards, and ships sailing on the ocean into purple vortexes.

But perhaps the strangest part about the store is the people here. There are a few of them, aside from Mom and me. They walk slowly. One woman picks up a vase, looks it over, then puts it back down only to pick it back up again. Another grabs a shirt off a tightly packed clothing rack. On the shirt is an image of someone wearing the same shirt.

Needless to say, I'm confused.

"Um, I know you love shopping in thrift stores, Mom, but do we really have time for this?" I finally ask.

I see Mom catch the eye of the woman behind the counter. She nods at Mom. Mom nods back, and then she turns to me.

"Here's what you do," she whispers to me. "Just grab any piece of clothing off the rack and go back into one of those dressing rooms."

Mom points to a row of three doors along the back wall of the store. "When you are inside, make sure the door is SECURELY FASTENED." She looks at me super serious. "Once you're sure it's SECURELY FASTENED, hang the piece of clothing on the wall."

"And then?" I ask.

"You'll see," says Mom.

You know, I wish Spy Academy were a little less cryptic.

Since I'm not actually trying on the piece of clothing, I grab just any shirt off the rack. As I make my way toward the back of the store, I notice some of the other customers whispering when I walk by. A few of them giggle.

Can this day get any weirder?

As Mom instructed, I make sure the dressing room door is *securely fastened*. Then I take a look around. The room is tiny and cramped—what a shock! I can barely fit myself in here, much less move around. I follow Mom's instructions exactly and hang the shirt on the hook on the well. There is a small **click**, and then I wait.

Nothing.

Is this some kind of spy test? Am I supposed to be patient? Am I supposed to click my heels three times and say "Spy Academy, Spy Academy"?

That's when I think, *What if I need to try the shirt on?*

I grab the shirt and look at it, hoping that maybe it's my size. And that's when I finally notice that it's not a shirt at all.

It's a clown suit. It looks just like you would

imagine. Pom-poms, suspenders, ruffles, you name it. There's even a big red wig safety-pinned to the shirt.

Just in case this is in fact a spy test, I put the clown costume on over my clothes. I'm just adjusting the wig when I hear another **click. click. click, click!**

The back wall of the dressing room starts to slide open. I step away, not knowing what to expect. It keeps going . . .

When the wall slides open completely, I see what looks like—could it be?—an elevator!

As soon as I step in, the wall slides closed behind me. Glancing to my left, I see that Mom is already in the elevator, still holding Agent Paul. She laughs. Again, I'd bet Agent

Paul is smiling too. That's when I remember: I'm dressed like a clown!

"While I can appreciate the art of disguise, you can wear your normal clothes," Mom says. "Part of being a spy is being patient. Once you heard the first click, you should have waited for something to happen."

Now she tells me! Feeling silly, I pull the costume off (remembering to take off the wig, too) and stuff it into my duffel bag. Speaking of my duffel bag, I have no clue how it got here—we didn't take it into the thrift store, but I know better than to ask. Which reminds me. How did Mom get in here, anyway?

As if she can read my mind, Mom says, "I came through the back wall of my dressing room. All three dressing rooms lead to this same elevator. Ready?"

Mom presses a button in the elevator. **DING!** But instead of going up or down, it speeds . . . sideways!

The elevator moves really fast, like I'm on the wackiest roller coaster of my life. Then, just as suddenly as it started, the elevator stops and sends me flying! I brace myself before bumping into the far wall.

"Mom! What is going—?"

Before I can finish my question, the elevator starts plunging downward. Mom, Agent Paul, and I hover a couple of inches above the floor for a few seconds before our feet drift back down. A few seconds later the elevator finally slows to a stop.

What had been the back wall of the dressing room slides open, and I can't believe my eyes.

Everywhere I look, I see another piece of high-tech equipment. Dozens of people are busy at work, scurrying from place to place. It's like a human beehive of activity, hidden deep underground.

"Welcome to Spy Academy!" Mom says. "Ready for the tour?"

Chapter Four

The Spy academy Tour

I HARDLY KNOW WHAT TO THINK OR SAY AS I FOLLOW Mom around. The size of the place alone is enough to make my head spin. Everywhere we walk it seems like a hallway or tunnel leads off to some secret hidden place, which would make sense, since this is a facility for spies, after all.

I can't believe it. If you'd have told me a week ago that I'd be inventing something for my mom the spy, I wouldn't have believed you. But horo I am!

Just as I start to wonder how long it took

Mom (and how long it will take me) to learn her way around this place, we come to a huge steel door, kind of like a bank vault.

"This is where you keep all the money, right?" I joke.

Mom smiles. "Everything you've seen so far only requires a level four clearance. Everything you'll see on the other side of this door requires a level seven clearance or higher."

"How many levels are there?" I ask.

"I'm sorry, Billy, that's classified."

She's serious!

Mom places her palm onto a smooth glass panel next to the door. The panel starts to glow. A small red light appears.

"Furry dog with one bone needs to be fed," she says.

The heavy steel door rises slowly, making a grinding sound.

"Is that 'furry dog' stuff some kind of secret code?" I ask.

"You're catching on," replies Mom.

When the door has vanished up into the

ceiling, we walk through the opening.

"'Furry dog' is my code name," Mom explains. "I picked that in honor of Philo. 'One bone' means I have one visitor with me. And 'needs to be fed' means that you are here for a briefing, to learn about your mission."

The steel door slides shut behind us. Mom leads me to another door, which swings open as we approach.

"This is our computer lab," she says as I follow her in. "Let's get you set up with a private agency network account."

The room is packed with row after row of people sitting at computers, typing away. After scanning the room, I notice that I'm not the only kid here. For some reason I expected everyone who works here to be an adult. I figured I would be a special case, being a young inventor and all.

But no, there are three kids that look to be about my age—two boys and a girl.

I guess I must be staring at them, because one of the boys looks up from his keyboard and says, "What, you thought you'd be the only kid here?"

I don't know what to say, so I just stand there with my mouth open, trying to get words to come out.

The kid laughs. "I'm just pulling your leg," he says. He's got long floppy black hair that keeps falling into his eyes. "I'm Josh. Welcome to Spy Academy!"

He points to the other boy, who is short with close-cropped brown hair.

"This is Drew," Josh says. "And this is Morgan."

He points to the girl with curly black hair whose face is buried in her keyboard.

"Hi, Drew. Hi, Morgan," I say. "I'm Billy."

"Billy's my son," Mom says. "So be nice! Billy, Agent Paul and I have to go take care of something. I'll be back in little bit." Mom leaves me with some orientation paperwork, like the school directory, and heads out of the lab.

"What's up, Billy?" says Drew, smiling and reaching his hand out to shake mine. There's something familiar about Drew that makes me feel more comfortable.

"Um, yeah, hi," Morgan mumbles, not bothering to look up.

"So what's your deal?" Josh asks me.

"Um, my 'deal'?" I reply. "I'm not sure what you mean."

"We all have something special about us that makes adults think we'd be good spies," Drew explains. "Like Josh here is a math whiz. Well, kind of. Watch."

Drew pulls out a calculator. Then he turns to Josh.

"Okay, Josh, what's 5,489 times 4,512?" he asks.

Drew types the numbers on the calculator. The answer comes up on the screen. He shows it to me. Josh closes his eyes for a second and then answers: "24,766,368."

I look down at the calculator again. Josh is right! Down to the last digit!

"You are a human calculator!" I cry. "That's amazing!"

After a second of silence, Josh and Drew burst out laughing. Morgan's mouth rises slightly in a kind of half smile.

"Nah," Josh says. "My actual 'deal' is even cooler than that. When people ask me a question, I can read their minds." My mouth drops open. Josh is a mind reader?!

"But it doesn't last very long," Josh continues. "I can only read minds when people ask me a direct question, or if I ask them a direct question. It's pretty cool, but it is limited."

I barely have a moment to wrap my head around this when Drew chimes in.

"And I have a photographic memory," he says.

"What do you mean?" I ask.

"Your mom was here for what, like, thirty seconds?" says Drew. "Here's what I remember. She was wearing black pants, black patent-leather shoes with little bows on them, a one-inch heel, a red-and-white printed shirt, and a black blazer with three gold buttons. She had a black leather purse with a strap that was worn out on the left side and was carrying a spiral notebook with a red cover, and her smartphone, which was in a navy-blue case. Here's a picture I took of her to prove it."

I'm not sure who I'm more impressed by—Josh or Drew. I was with Mom all morning, and honestly, if anyone asked me what she was wearing, I wouldn't have a clue. All I know is she wasn't wearing a clown suit like me.

I turn to Morgan.

"What about you?" I ask, thinking she must be equally as cool. "What's your deal?"

Morgan doesn't answer. I look back at Josh and Drew. Josh just shrugs.
"She's working on some big project," he says. "But don't underestimate her. Morgan is really strong and superfast—she's like a ninja!"

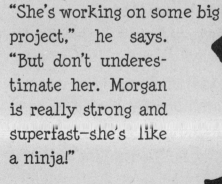

"Yeah, don't mess with Morgan," Drew agrees.

Josh continues. "She's also awesome with languages. She speaks eight fluently. Right, Mo? MO?" Josh shouts.

Morgan finally looks up, sighs, and rolls her eyes.

"*Déjame en paz*," Morgan says. "That's Spanish."

"*Lasciami in pace.* That's Italian."

"*Lass mich alleine.* That's German. Can I stop now or do you need to hear the other four languages?"

"Um, just the English translation would be great," I say.

"I wish you would LEAVE ME ALONE!" she replies. "How's that for a translation?" Then she looks back down and returns to her work. Josh and Drew howl with laughter.

"Okay, Billy. Your turn," says Josh. "What's your deal?"

"I guess my deal is that I'm good at inventing things," I say, and wonder if that sounds incredibly boring, especially because Manny runs a lot of our business. "You might've heard of some of my inventions, like the All Ball or the STINK SPECTACULAR?"

"You're the kid who invented the All Ball?" Drew exclaims. "I never go anywhere without my All Ball! I love it! I think it's the coolest invention ever!"

He reaches into his backpack and pulls out the small model, then tosses it into the air and catches it a couple of times as it changes from baseball to tennis ball to golf ball. "You really invented this?"

I never like to assume that anyone has heard of me. Still, I've been all over TV for a

while now. Then again, maybe spies don't have enough time to watch TV.

"Uh, yeah, that's me," I admit.

At that moment Mom pops back into the computer lab.

"Come on, Billy," she says. "Time to get you set up in your room, and you'll get to meet your roommate."

"See you guys later," I say as I follow Mom out.

That's when it hits me.

Roommate?

I hadn't even thought about that. A roommate. I mean, at home I share an office with Manny, but we're best friends. What if this roommate and I don't get along?

And suddenly I no longer feel like a great inventor on the adventure of his life. I'm back to being just an anxious kid.

Chapter Five

Roommates and Table Mates

THE LIVING AREA AT SPY ACADEMY LOOKS PRETTY much like my bunk at Camp Lots O' Activities. It even has the same lingering scent of old campfires and slimy lake water, which is strange because we're underground.

We stop in front of a wooden door. I can feel the butterflies in my stomach—my leg starts to twitch too, which sometimes happens when I'm anxious.

Mom knocks on the door.

"What's the password?" booms a deep voice from inside the room.

I wait for my mom to bust out another code.

"Open the door, Xavier," Mom calls out, shaking her head and rolling her eyes.

"Do you have your tickets?" the voice comes back.

"This is not the ballpark, Xavier," Mom says. "It's a dorm room. Open the door."

A few seconds later the door swings open, and there stands my roommate. Or, I should say, *towers* my roommate. According to Mom, he's a year older than me, but he's at least a foot taller. And he looks like he just stepped off the cover of a sports magazine. He's got

muscles everywhere. He's got so many muscles, I almost don't even notice his Hyenas T-shirt. The Hyenas are my favorite baseball team. But this guy looks like he should be *playing* for them, not wearing their T-shirt!

"Xavier, I'd like you to meet—"

Before Mom can finish introducing me, her phone beeps with an incoming message.

"*ACK!*" she exclaims. "I'm sorry, Billy, I have an emergency situation I have to deal with." Then she mutters really quickly—something about Agent Paul. Without another word, she turns and races down the hall.

I smile at Xavier, wondering if he can tell how nervous I am.

"Hi, I'm Billy Sure. Nice to meet you," I say.

Xavier looks me up and down. "So, you're the great inventor, huh?" he says. Then he *snorts*. The sound is somewhere between a scoff and a laugh, but I'm not sure which.

I ignore his snort and walk into the room. The walls on Xavier's side are covered with sports posters—baseball, football, basketball, and hockey, all with players making spectacular moves. Each person on the posters looks as muscular as Xavier. In fact, one of them might even *be* Xavier!

My side of the room, on the other hand, is

bare. There's a small bed, a desk, a dresser, and some blank cinder-block walls. I wish I'd brought some pictures with me. Maybe the photo of me and Manny next to the All Ball could make this dorm room a little cheerier.

"So, you're a Hyenas fan?" I ask Xavier, in an attempt at some kind of conversation. "I am too. In fact, I'm friends with Carl Bourette." Carl Bourette, the Hyenas' shortstop, is a big fan of Sure Things, Inc. He even guest starred on our TV special to find Sure Things' Next Big Thing, which was awesome!

"Uh-huh," Xavier says. Then he sits at his desk and starts writing.

"What are you working on?" I ask.

"Code breaking," Xavier replies. "It's one of the classes you'll—well, the *real* spies in training, I mean—take."

At least he answered me. Still, he doesn't seem too friendly.

I sit on my bed and stare at the blank wall. I thought I'd be spending time with Mom, but she's hardly been around. I thought I'd be inventing immediately, but it looks like that's not happening. And Xavier doesn't seem to be too pleased that he's stuck with me as a roommate.

I'll admit it. Aside from meeting Josh, Morgan, and Drew, Spy Academy has just been a confusing blur.

I decide to do something other than sit around and feel sorry for myself. I open my bag, pull out my laptop, and type out an e-mail to Manny. I wish I had more to say, but since I'm not in Barbados and I can't describe anything where I am, the e-mail is pretty short.

Hi partner,

Just got to Barbados. Miss you. Hope
school and work are good, and things are
okay with Emily.

—Billy

I hit send and wait for the reply.

A few hours later, when dinnertime rolls
around, there's still no response from Manny.
Which is weird, because if I know Manny, he
is on his smartphone 24-7. Part of me feels
a little jealous—what is Manny doing that's
better than answering e-mails from his
business partner and best friend?

To top it off, I notice that Xavier has left
the room. I must have taken a nap and didn't
hear him go, and it's not like he said good-bye
or anything. He certainly didn't ask me if I
wanted to sit with him at dinner. I'm hun-
gry, so I get up out of bed and head toward
the dining room . . . alone. I've never been
super popular at school (even being super

famous), but I've always at least had Manny on my side.

Thankfully, as soon as I walk into the dining room, I hear my name.

"Hey, Billy! Over here. Come sit with us."

I look across the room and see Drew waving to me. He's sitting at a table with Josh and Morgan. His smile is big and toothy, and I instantly feel at ease.

"Thanks, Drew," I say, dragging over a chair from another table. "I'll grab some food and be right back."

Okay, so maybe my roommate situation isn't great, and my best friend is ignoring my e-mails, but at least I have three new friends!

As I push my tray along the food line, my spirits start to pick up. I remember a conversation I had with my cousin when I visited him at college. He told me that it's not a terrible thing if your roommate is not your pal, as long as you have good friends at school. Drew's invitation turns my whole mood around.

The food in the cafeteria is amazing. It's not

normal cafeteria food, like mac and cheese or chicken fingers (even though chicken fingers aren't really "normal" food, either—everyone knows CHICKEN FINGERS DAY is the best at Fillmore, so people go kind of crazy). Anyway, the theme of the night is breakfast for dinner, and the food has names like "exploding eggs" and "self-destruct cereal."

"Why do they call them 'exploding eggs'?" I ask when I return to the table. I scoop up my first forkful of eggs and wait for my new friends' explanation.

Suddenly, Drew jumps up and tries to whisk my fork away, but he's too late. All of a sudden,

there's a *pop!* and the eggs **EXPLODE!**

Morgan sighs.

"Spies always have to be on their toes and think fast," she says. "There's no hesitation allowed. Watch."

Without even asking me if it's okay, and wasting no time, Morgan grabs a fork and shoves some of my exploding eggs into her mouth. Or at least I think she does. One second a forkful of food is on my plate, the next second it's gone.

Morgan really is like a ninja!

I try to imitate Morgan, but I just make a mess of things. Drew and Josh can't stop laughing at the literal egg on my face.

"You ready for classes tomorrow, Billy?" asks Josh as the last bite of my food pops away.

"I guess," I reply. "When my mom asked

me to come here to help invent something, I never thought I'd actually be studying real spy stuff."

"It's really fun," says Drew. "I love analyzing evidence and practicing surveillance techniques. I even love interrogating bad guys. Scratch that. I *really* love interrogating bad guys!"

"Will we really do that?" I ask.

"Most of the time they bring in an actor to pretend to be an enemy spy," Drew explains. "They give him a fake secret which we have to get out of him."

"Or her," Morgan says quietly.

Morgan is really interesting. She appears to like hanging out with these two, yet she doesn't really try to be part of any conversation. Until times like now, when she speaks up.

"Drew's right," she continues. "Usually they bring in an actor to play the bad guy, but every once in a while, when real agents are working on a case, they toss in a real bad guy."

Is she saying this just to scare me? I don't really know, but she seems excited when she says it.

"Really?" I ask.

"Really," she replies, flashing the warmest, most genuine smile I've seen her show in the little time I've known her. She is an odd one, all right.

"I can't wait to see the invention lab," I admit, trying to steer the conversation toward something I'm a little more comfortable with. After all, my mission is to create the Spy Dye. I haven't even started on the blueprints! "Have you guys ever been in there?"

"Not me," says Josh. "I'm strictly a computer geek. You'll find me in the computer lab working away. If only I could read computers' minds!"

"Actually, I work in the invention lab," says Drew. "It's pretty cool. It has everything you might need to invent stuff. And, if I must say so myself—"

"You must," Morgan chimes in, "because no one else will."

"Ah, yeah, what I was going to say," Drew continues, "is that I've dabbled a bit with inventing. I've had some modest success. I'd love to see your work once you get rolling in the lab, Billy. If that's okay, of course."

"Sure," I say, although I don't really know what I'm getting myself into, working in a strange lab with parts that I didn't gather, away from the comfort of my own workbench. "As soon as I figure out what I'm doing, you're welcome to come take a look."

Drew smiles. The table gets quiet. I finish my dessert—erupting lava cake, which is delicious but also scary—and realize how sleepy I am.

"Well, guys, it's been a long day," I say, standing up. "First day of school tomorrow. I'm going to get some sleep. See ya in class."

I head out of the dining room, tired. It's hard to believe that I only left home this morning. It feels like I've been at this place for a week already.

I step into my dorm room and see Xavier working on his code breaking homework. Only now he also has four different baseball games streaming in small windows on his computer monitor.

He doesn't acknowledge the fact that I'm back in the room. It makes me really miss Manny. In fact, talking with so many other people just makes me miss Manny in general. Even when Manny is so engrossed in work, he always acknowledges that I'm there. Maybe I'll write Manny another e-mail. That should make me feel better.

I sit down at my computer and bring up Manny's e-mail address.

Hey partner,

Just got in from a great day at the beach and thought I'd shoot off another note to you.

How's it going, working with Emily? If I know you guys, the No-Trouble Bubble will be ready for production in no time. Is she being too grumpy? If so, tell her I said "Stop!" Like she listens to me . . . lol.

Hey, you know what? Since my inventor's brain never stops working, even when I'm supposed to be on vacation, I think I've come up with an idea! What do you think of the Instant Sand Castle Maker? I think it will help kids on beaches everywhere come up with awesome sand castles. We'll talk about it when I get back, but I think we could have this invention ready for next summer.

Anyway, gotta go. Mom says hi and so do I.

—Billy

I hit send.
I was right. I do feel better after writing to

Manny, even if I am making all this stuff up. I mean, the Instant Sand Castle Maker isn't a *terrible* idea. I could definitely see it becoming the new cool thing at beaches everywhere!

I look over a list of my classes, waiting for a reply from Manny. Usually he replies to e-mails instantly, but, like before, I hear nothing back.

Exhausted, I crawl into bed.

Chapter Six

The Invention Lab

WHEN I WAKE UP THE NEXT MORNING, THE FIRST thing I do is check my e-mail. Still no replies from Manny. I rub my eyes and get dressed. I should be focusing on inventing Spy Dye and starting classes, but I'm a little concerned that I haven't heard from him.

I head out the door and meet up with Josh, Drew, and Morgan for breakfast.

"We have a free period before first class," Drew says in between bites of his detonating doughnut. *CHOMP!* "I always spend my time in the invention lab. It sounds like you might want to too. You should come with me."

I'm suddenly really glad I'm friends with Drew. I mean, I was already glad to be friends with Drew, but even more so now because he's an inventor.

After breakfast Drew walks me down the hall to the invention lab.

"I bet it's really cool working at Sure Things, Inc.," he says. "You and Manny must be a great team."

"We are," I admit. I don't think I remember mentioning Manny before, but I've been so nervous, it probably slipped out.

Thankfully, the invention lab helps calm my nerves. Just the smell of it all is enough to lift my spirits!

There are a few inventors already at their workbenches. Everyone has a different style. Some workstations are messy; some are neat. One guy's workstation only has red items on it. Another woman is piecing together a giant dog bone.

Drew and I stop by one of the inventor's

workstations. The inventor has white hair that sticks out from his head in every direction. He looks a bit like Albert Einstein. There are dresses scattered all around him. And baby clothes?

"Billy, meet Julius," Drew says. "Julius invented CLOTHES IN A CAN."

Julius smiles. "Want to see?" he asks.

"Of course!" I say. I'm intrigued. What are Clothes in a Can?

Without saying a word, Julius picks up a spray can. **PFFFFT!** He sprays it at me. It kind of tickles. Kind of like Philo is licking my face!

When the tickling stops, I look down and see that I am now wearing a three-piece rainbow suit and a checkered tie. Julius sprays me again, and I'm suddenly in a full scuba outfit.

My whole body is covered in black rubber. I'm even wearing flippers!

One more spray and I'm wearing a sweat suit, complete with wrist and head sweatbands. A final spray and my original T-shirt and jeans return.

"Very handy for undercover agents who have to make quick changes," Julius says, while Drew smiles and nods vigorously.

"Nice work," I say, happy to be back in my own clothes.

We move to the next workstation. There I meet a woman who has multicolored stripes in her hair and is wearing a traditional long white lab coat.

"I'm Sylvia," she says. "Nice to meet you, Billy. I've invented the PALM POWER 5000. It turns your hands into their own source of electricity. Here."

Sylvia places a small device into my hand. It is about half the size of a cell phone.

"Touch this lamp," she says, pointing to a table lamp that is unplugged.

Ding! I touch the lamp with my hand and the bulb lights up.

"Try this," she says next. "I'm about to make a strawberry-banana smoothie."

I touch a blender on Sylvia's workbench, just as she calls out, "OH, NO! WAIT!"

The blender whirs to life, spinning the fruit and yogurt Sylvia had put in—but there's no lid!

Whirp! Whirp! Whirp! Chunks of banana, pieces of strawberry, and big splats of yogurt go flying out of the blender. I take my hand off and the blender stops, but not before Sylvia is covered in her gooey breakfast.

"Sorry," I say sheepishly.

"My fault. I forgot the lid," Sylvia says, wiping some red mush from her rainbow-colored hair. "Welcome to the lab. Crazy stuff happens here all the time."

I'm beginning to like these inventors.

Drew and I move on. I'm surprised to see my roommate Xavier at the next workstation.

"Hey, roomie, how's it going?" he asks,

seeming much friendlier than before. Maybe, like me, the lab is his happy place.

"What are you working on?" I ask. I'm not even sure I realized that Xavier was an inventor.

"HIDDEN INK, for sending secret messages," he says. "Well, I've actually already invented that and am working on something else, but I'll show you Hidden Ink because it's cool."

"Hidden Ink? Oh, you mean like with lemon juice and water?" I ask. I did a science experiment at Fillmore Middle where I had to make invisible ink. It worked for the most part—but the ink made the paper bumpy, so you could tell it wasn't completely blank.

"Nope, that recipe, and all the others like that can still be seen on the paper, even though the ink appears to be invisible," Xavier explains. "My formula for Hidden Ink is COMPLETELY UNDETECTABLE. I'll demonstrate. Go ahead and write something."

He hands me a blank piece of paper and a

pen. I start to write a short message, but nothing comes out of the pen.

"I can't tell if it's working," I say.

"Just go ahead and write something," he says.

I finish, but there is still nothing on the paper . . . or not that I can see.

Xavier takes the paper and holds it up to a lightbulb. My words suddenly appear:

This place is pretty cool.

The exact words I wrote.

"Hidden Ink can only be read when it is very close to a light," Drew explains.

Xavier moves the paper away from the bulb and the writing instantly disappears. I'm impressed!

Drew and I continue on toward the back of the lab.

"The desks are arranged alphabetically, so we'll be sitting next to each other," Drew explains, pointing to an empty workstation. A sign above it reads: BiLLY SURE. Drew settles into the station next to me, which says DREW S. It's kind of weird that my sign has a last name and Drew's just has an initial, but it's probably just 'cause no one knows me yet. I'm here, and now it's time to get to work!

And that's when I notice that something is wrong.

The place is immaculate. There's not a tool or part or anything on the desk's surface. The drawers and shelves that surround me all have perfectly printed labels. I pull open a drawer labeled TOOLS and see a line of tools placed precisely in size order.

How am I supposed to work in this environment? I mean, it's okay for other people, but

Billy Sure

this looks like it was designed by a neat-freak!

As I open drawers and pull stuff off shelves, I start to realize that yeah, I miss my own familiar workspace, but really I miss having Manny right there in the same room with me.

Doing my best to shake off these feelings, I get to work.

After an hour Drew stops by my desk. "How's the progress going?" he asks.

"It's going . . . slowly," I admit, although "slowly" doesn't really cover it. My Spy Dye looks kind of like old soup. Probably because it *is* old soup.

"Well, are you ready for your first class, Billy?" Drew asks. "Interrogation. Things can get pretty wild in there."

"Okay," I say. Interrogation? Bring it on!

Chapter Seven

To Catch a Scammer

IN CLASS I TAKE A SEAT NEAR MY NEW FRIENDS. THE teacher, Mr. Doval, doesn't make a fuss over me, like teachers do back at Fillmore when there's a new kid. *Phew.*

Mr. Doval stands up and speaks. "There are a few basic interrogation techniques I'd like to outline for you," he says. "Of course, we do not condone hurting those we interrogate. However, a little discomfort can go a long way."

Mr. Doval presses a button on his desk. *ZURP!* A light blazes, shining up from the surface.

Then a life-size hologram of a man in an orange prison jumpsuit stands in front of the classroom!

WOW!

"In this case, Prisoner A, as we'll call him, has information about the agency's missing iguana," Mr. Doval says. "Watch as we demonstrate the use of basic physical discomfort to gain what we need."

Iguana? Before I can ask why the agency has an iguana, a hologram guard brings Prisoner A a tall glass of iced tea. *SLURP!* The prisoner drinks it down quickly.

This doesn't look so bad to me. In fact, I'm pretty thirsty, myself.

We wait. A few seconds later, the guard brings out another glass of iced tea. And again,

Prisoner A drinks it down. This is repeated two more times, and that's when I notice that with each glass the prisoner drinks, his body language changes. He appears more and more uncomfortable.

The prisoner's legs move closer together, his arms wrap around his body, and he grits his teeth.

Oh! I get the "discomfort" that Mr. Doval was talking about now. They're not going to let Prisoner A go to the bathroom after drinking all that iced tea! And let me tell you . . . that was a *lot* of iced tea. I've been there on long car rides. Long car rides where Emily knows I have to pee and will talk about waterfalls and swimming pools and anything to make me go crazy. Yup, I would talk too, if it meant that someone would give me a bathroom key!

The hologram vanishes.

"Physical discomfort," says Mr. Doval. "Any questions?"

No one raised a hand. The example couldn't have been more clear.

"This next technique is especially interesting. We call it COVER STORY. It involves making a suspect repeat the tiny details of a false story he or she has been telling, again and again, until you catch the suspect in a lie."

Now, this is something Drew and his memory would be good at.

"Watch this next demonstration," Mr. Doval says.

But we don't watch his next demonstration. Because just as he is about to press a button on his desk, the classroom door opens and in walks . . . Mom!

Mom is followed by two other agents. They lead a teenage girl in front of them.

"Sorry to interrupt, Mr. Doval," she begins, as the agents guide the girl over to a seat in front of the classroom. "But I have a suspect here that I think your class might benefit from interrogating."

"She's probably an actor," Josh whispers to me.

"Actually, this suspect is real, not an actor," Mom says.

I think Mom's special agent superpower is her hearing.

"This young woman is a suspect in an online scam," Mom explains. "The scam promises a magic cream that will help kids grow taller. Kids buy it and then never receive it." She turns to the suspect. "What do you call it?"

"I don't know what you're talking about," she says.

"Class, could you help me interrogate this suspect to find out if she is the scammer? Good luck!"

Then Mom leaves the classroom.

To my shock, Morgan jumps up from her seat and hurries to the front of the room. She stares at the suspect. The suspect stares back. I can't tell what either of them must be thinking.

Then Morgan points to something on the suspect's T-shirt. I lean in to see if I can read what it says, but the letters are unfamiliar. Greek, maybe?

Morgan starts speaking in Greek. The

suspect's eyes light up with surprise. (Later, Morgan explains what she said to her, so here's how it went down.)

"It is nice to meet someone else who speaks Greek. I have to tell you I feel pretty bad for you. I can't stand the people in this room. I don't like anything about this whole place. I'm being forced to stay here. But you look like someone I can trust."

As she speaks in Greek, I can see the teenager start to relax. She looks a lot less nervous. Morgan continues:

"If you can tell me what really happened, I can help you fool these people and get you out of here. What do you think? And don't worry, no one else here speaks Greek. They'll have no idea what you are saying."

The suspect's whole facial expression changes. She gives Morgan a small smile. Morgan turns her back to the suspect, looks right at Josh, and gives him a signal with her eyebrows. Josh leans forward in his seat.

"So, what were you planning to do with the money raised from people buying your product?" Morgan asks.

The suspect speaks slowly in Greek, seeming to get more and more comfortable as she goes along.

Josh puts his fingers to his temples and shuts his eyes tightly. A few seconds later, Josh whispers something to Drew. They're really in sync. It's awesome. Morgan sits down. Drew walks up to the front of the room.

"Tell me what exactly you were trying to do with your business?" Drew asks the suspect.

"I was raising money for college," she says.

"But isn't it true that the kids who ordered your magic growing cream never got it?" Drew asks.

"Well, we did have some shipping problems," she replies nervously.

"Shipping from a warehouse, correct?"

"Yeah."

"Well, we contacted the warehouse, and they've never heard of your magic growing cream." Drew is holding the suspect's file in his hand. Wow. He must have read that pretty quickly!

The girl squirms in her seat.

Drew leans in close. "Why did you want to buy a red car?" he asks quickly.

"I wanted to impress . . . I mean, what car?"

"The cherry-red convertible sports car with turbo-charged engine, eight-speaker sound system, 5-speed transmission with overdrive, Bluetooth, and voice-controlled GPS? That car."

"How—how did you know all that?" the girl

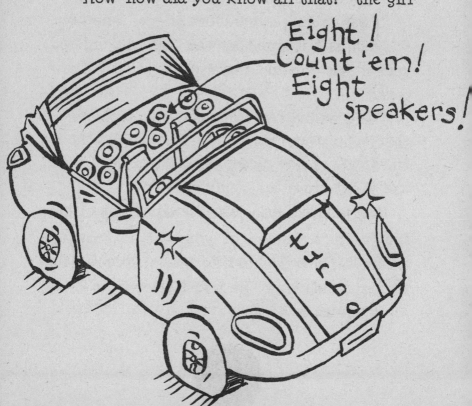

stammers, obviously stunned by the detail of Drew's description.

"So it's true," Drew replies.

The girl buries her head in her hands. "Yes, it's true. There was no real project. My website was just a way to scam money out of kids so I could buy a cool car. Everyone else at school has a car, but not me!"

Drew turns to the two agents who brought the suspect in with Mom.

"Agents, I think you have your confession," he says. "The suspect is all yours."

The agents lead the girl from the room.

I am amazed. How did that just happen?

"Excellent work, Morgan, Josh, and Drew," says Mr. Doval. "Would you all please come to the front of the classroom and explain your use of interrogation techniques?"

Morgan and Josh join Drew in front of the class.

"When I saw the Greek writing on the girl's shirt, I figured I could play good cop with her by speaking to her in Greek," Morgan explains.

"Once Morgan asked her a direct question, I could read her mind," Josh says, picking up the story. "Her thoughts about the car were in Greek, but she pictured the car in her mind. I whispered the details to Drew, who remembered them all thanks to his great memory."

"And I used a variation of the cover story technique. I threw out the true details of the car to shock her into messing up her story and finally confessing," Drew says.

"Excellent work," says Mr. Doval. "Thank you all! Class dismissed."

As we all get up, I head to the front of the room.

"You guys are amazing!" I say.

"Stick with us, kid," says Morgan. "You'll learn a lot."

Before I can comment on Morgan calling me "kid" even though we are the same age, Mom comes bursting in. She looks anxious, upset, and out of breath.

"Mom, what's the matter?" I ask.

She pulls me aside.

"Billy, I've just been handed an assignment that requires the Spy Dye ASAP!" she explains. "Agent Paul and I need your help. You are the only one who can invent Spy Dye—even if you have to use your sleep-inventing technique."

"But what about my classes?" I ask. I'm actually looking forward to seeing Drew, Josh, and Morgan in action again after what they just pulled off.

"No more classes for you today, I'm afraid," Mom explains. "I was hoping that you could ease into this place, take all your classes to get a context for the Spy Dye, and then hit the invention lab to work on it." Mom shakes her head. "But it looks like you are going to have to fast-track the inventing. We have to go to the lab. Now."

Chapter Eight

The Big Rescue Mission

BACK AT THE INVENTION LAB, I GRAB SOME MATERIALS from the supply closet and spread them out on my workbench. To be honest, I didn't really look at what I was grabbing. I feel more at home that way.

The invention lab is a lot less crowded than it was this morning, probably because a lot of the kids—like Drew and Xavier—are in class. I see Julius and Sylvia, though. We wave to each other.

I'm optimistic that the Spy Dye will be easy to invent. That's because this invention is like a mash-up of my other ones. The All Ball can change into different shapes—just like Spy Dye will help to conceal gear by making it look like something else. The No-Trouble Bubble can protect someone from danger—just like Spy Dye. And with the mind reading capability of the Best Test, I can make the Spy Dye operate on command. . . .

BOOM!

Just as I'm thinking about how easy all this will be, there's a big flash of lightning, and Sylvia's workstation gets charred!

"I'm okay!" Sylvia shouts immediately. I walk over to her.

"What happened?" I ask. Sylvia's hair is sticking straight up. It's like she created a personal lightning storm!

"Oh, it's just the Palm Power 5000," Sylvia replies. "I'm having some trouble with it. It's just too strong. And of course, we need it for the Big Rescue Mission!"

"THE BIG RESCUE MISSION?" I repeat.

"There's an agent being held captive by enemy spies," Sylvia explains. "And it's pretty serious. I have to complete the Palm Power 5000 ASAP. Without it—and other inventions— we might not be able to rescue our agent."

Uh-oh. I get that sick feeling in my stomach whenever I'm under pressure. My feet start tapping. Mom told me she needs the Spy Dye ASAP too. Is my invention supposed to save an agent from enemy spies?

Sylvia starts to clean her workbench, but it's all fried. It kind of smells like my Dad's cooking on those rare times he admits that something went wrong. But to my surprise, Sylvia takes out a spray bottle from the supply closet and sprays something all over her stuff. Instantly it turns back into how it was before the fire!

"BURN SPRAY," Sylvia explains, probably noticing how confused I look. "It's a special blend I came up with. When you have an invention that creates tons of electricity, it helps being able to reverse the damage of frying."

As Sylvia spritzes the Burn Spray on her things—her workbench, her paperwork, her supplies—they begin to bubble for a second and then come back to life. Everything, well, except for . . .

"Sylvia?" I ask, a little shy. "I think . . . I think you might need to spray your hair, too." I'm a little nervous, because I'm definitely not somebody who comments on others' appearances. But I think Sylvia might want to fix the hair that got burned by her Palm Power 5000. She looks kind of like a mad scientist, which I suppose she is.

Sylvia chuckles.

"Oh, that," she says, smiling, and sprays her hair. Instantly it's back to normal!

I don't know about you, but I think Burn Spray is really cool.

But I'll tell you what isn't cool: pressure. I'm kind of used to it by now, because of school and work and inventing and everything. But I've never been in a position where one of my inventions is supposed to help save someone on a rescue mission. And after talking to Sylvia, I think that is exactly what Spy Dye is supposed to do!

I get back to my workstation and line it with test tubes and beakers. I start by filling them with black, brown, red, and blond hair coloring. Cranking up flames under the beakers, I bring the liquid to a boil. SERIOUSLY, DON'T TRY THIS AT HOME.

I'm about to add a secret mixture I used for the All Ball, when I hear a hum from several workstations away. The hum gets louder and louder.

Looking in the direction of the noise, I see Sylvia still at her workstation, attempting to add some enhancements to her Palm Power 5000. She is now frantically trying to adjust the device. I see a look of panic on her face.

ZZZZZZaP!

A jagged bolt of electricity goes shooting out of the Palm Power 5000 and slams right into my workstation. The test tubes full of hair dye explode and blend into a goopy pool of colors not usually found in nature.

"I am so sorry, Billy," Sylvia says as she races over to my workstation. "Are you all right?"

"I'm okay," I say. My Spy Dye, on the other hand . . .

Sylvia tries to fix it with her Burn Spray, but it doesn't help. I look down at the colorful mess and see that it has hardened into a blob. I can pick the whole thing up in once piece.

Sylvia shakes her Burn Spray a few times and tries spraying again.

"I think maybe Burn Spray only fixes

things that know what they're supposed to be," I suggest. "But my Spy Dye probably didn't work. So Burn Spray doesn't know how to form that again." I toss the blob back and forth between my hands and then toss it into the trash can. I miss, but barely, and get up to put it in.

"Again, I'm so sorry," Sylvia apologizes, and returns to her workbench to figure out what went wrong with her device.

After some more unsuccessful attempts at inventing Spy Dye, I hear my stomach start to rumble. *Grrrr!* That's when I realize something— it's past dinnertime! The cafeteria must be serving dessert by now!

I get up and walk to the exit, which is just past Xavier's workstation. Maybe I'll invite him to dessert with me. But that's when I realize something else, too—classes are over, and it looks like Xavier never even stopped by.

I scurry to the cafeteria just in time for dessert. Morgan, Josh, and Drew are at their usual table, scooping shattering sherbet into their mouths. I'm hoping that it's the sherbet that shatters and not that the sherbet shatters your teeth!

"Billy!" Drew says when he sees me. "We missed you in the rest of our classes today!"

"I missed you guys too," I say. "You all were incredible in interrogation!"

I might be imagining it, but Morgan's mouth turns up into a slight smile.

"How's the inventing going?" Drew asks.

"Not so good," I admit. "I'm having no success in the lab, so I think I'm going to have to try sleep-inventing tonight."

"Sleep-inventing?" Drew asks.

"Yeah, I know it sounds weird, but that's what I do," I say. "Some people sleepwalk or sleep-eat. I sleep-invent. It's how I've come up with a lot of inventions. So maybe it will work for Spy Dye, too."

Drew nods. He's an inventor too, so I think that's why he gets it.

After dinner, back in my room, I check my e-mail. There's got to be a message from Manny.

But there isn't. No e-mail replies, no texts—nothing. Is Manny okay?

Xavier isn't back in the room either. I just can't figure that guy out. At first he didn't want any part of me. Now he seems to have disappeared.

I get ready for bed. Hoping for the best, I slip my pen under my pillow and place a fresh sheet of paper on my desk. I'm ready to write some blueprints for the Spy Dye in my sleep. It's been a long day. It doesn't take me long to fall fast asleep.

Chapter Nine

The Missing Blueprints

WHEN I WAKE UP IN THE MORNING, I'M SHOCKED. I can't believe my eyes! There is nothing on the paper. Nothing. ZILCH.

My pen is at my desk, though, so I obviously got up, took the pen, and sat at my desk last night. I have a really strong feeling that I invented Spy Dye last night. But since there are no blueprints... a frightening thought strikes me:

Did someone steal the blueprints I wrote up and swap them for this blank piece of paper?

But who would do anything like that? And why?

I immediately look over at Xavier's bed, but once again, he must have come in after I fell asleep and gotten up before I even woke up. But why would Xavier want to mess with me?

This is the point where, had this conversation been taking place with Manny instead of just in my head, he would've said something like: "No point worrying about this before we have some facts."

And so, with Manny's voice echoing in my head, I push these paranoid thoughts aside and get ready for my day.

At breakfast I meet up with Drew, Josh, and Morgan. Breakfast today is crying crepes. I'm kind of getting the hang of the whole wasting-no-time-from-plate-to-mouth thing, because the crepes only cry tearfully at me once. Some of the other students aren't so lucky and the cries echo like a baby. *WAH WAH! WAH!*

News about the Big Rescue Mission seems to have traveled fast, but no one knows what it's all about.

"I'm going to find out," Morgan vows. "I

stayed up all night thinking about how I can use my ninja skills to help."

"Yeah, and I stayed up asking the teachers questions, hoping to read their minds!" Josh says.

"None of the details I've noticed are any help," Drew says.

"What about you, Billy?" Josh asks. "Any sleep?"

"Uh," I say. I have to admit, this makes me feel kind of bad. I slept without a problem last night. "A little," I say sheepishly. "I really hoped to have the Spy Dye blueprints when I woke up. But my blueprints were blank."

"Blank," Drew repeats and closes his eyes, as if he's thinking really hard about why that could be.

Just then there's a high-pitched *WAH! WAH! WAH!* from the other side of the cafeteria. Sounds like someone else didn't get their crying oreos into their mouth fast enough!

"I really can't take that noise anymore,"

Drew says. "I'll see you guys in class. Later."
He gets up and leaves.

I work at the lab during free period, but there's
no luck there. Spy Dye keeps turning into a
blob—a gross, slimy blob too, made up of hair
dye and guacamole (don't ask).

I know I have to get this invention to Mom
ASAP, but maybe what I really need is to clear
my head for a bit. I decide to march over to
today's class—surveillance techniques. My
chair near Josh, Morgan, and Drew is open, so I
sit down there, and we wave to each other as I
pass by. After a few moments, Mr. Doval walks
in for our lesson.

"The most basic form of surveillance is
simply following suspects as they walk along
the street," Mr. Doval begins. "But this is not
as simple as it sounds. In this type of surveillance, the suspect has the greatest chance
of realizing that he or she is being followed.
Thankfully, we have some more advanced
techniques."

Mr. Doval presses a button on the top of the shiny black desk, and a holographic image comes to life and plays out in three dimensions in front of the classroom!

A man in a long trench coat, a fedora, and dark glasses walks quickly down a city street. Honestly, I have to bite my tongue to keep from giggling.

This is how I pictured myself in my dream about being a spy the night before I left to come here. I got the image from old black-and-white movies that I like to watch with Dad sometimes. The teachers at Spy Academy should really update their holo-films.

Trench coat man glances back over his shoulder every few steps. He obviously thinks he's being followed.

"If you were to simply walk along the street behind the suspect, it wouldn't take him long to realize that he's being followed," Mr. Doval says. "Here are a few techniques you can use to avoid being noticed."

As trench coat man hurries along the

sidewalk, I see a woman on a bicycle in the street nearby. She doesn't look like she's following him, though. In fact, she looks a little flustered! She gets caught in traffic, falls behind him, talks on her phone with her boyfriend about being late to YODELING CLASS, and asks someone for directions.

"The other major area of surveillance we use is remote surveillance," Mr. Doval continues. "These techniques include hidden video cameras and TV surveillance trucks. Our surveillance units work closely with our evidence analysis units to create air-tight cases against those who would do us harm."

"Isn't that what Agent Paul was doing?" asks Morgan. "Surveillance? But he was caught."

I see Mr. Doval's lips stretch into a thin line. He looks kind of scared.

"Agent Paul is one of the best employees we have—octopus or human," he says curtly. "And anything you've heard about The Big Rescue Mission—"

I gasp. Morgan vowed to find out what the

rescue mission is all about, and it looks like she did! Agent Paul must be the agent who was caught by enemy spies! Mom mentioned that she and Agent Paul are a team. Kind of like how Manny and me are a team. Which means . . . if I don't invent Spy Dye, Agent Paul *and* my mom are in BIG TROUBLE!

So much for class being a place to clear my head. Now I'm feeling the pressure big time.

"—doesn't concern you," Mr. Doval continues. "The Big Rescue Mission is for talented, fully-fledged spies only. But don't worry. You'll get there someday."

A silence washes over the class now.

That's when it hits me. Of course Josh, Drew, and Morgan will get there someday. They'll be out on missions saving people. But me? I'm about as useful at scammer catching as I am at dancing, and that is to say, not very useful. I'm here for one reason and one reason only—and that's to invent Spy Dye and save Agent Paul.

I can't exactly get up and leave the class room, so my mind starts to wander. All my thoughts about Spy Dye keep coming back to Xavier. Could he possibly have moved my pen and prevented me from sleep-inventing?

I'm so busy thinking that I hardly notice we've finished the lesson on surveillance. Some spy I am.

"Our next lesson is in calming yourself to the point where your pulse rate doesn't change when you tell a lie. This—along with monitoring your breath and sweat—allows you to fool a lie detector," Mr. Doval says, bringing me out of my thoughts.

"I'll try this one," says Morgan. She bounds up to the front of the room.

Morgan sits in a chair next to a lie detector machine. Mr. Doval wraps a blood-pressure cuff around her arm and clips a pulse-measuring device to her finger.

The wires from these clips connect to a big machine with a roll of thin white paper and a needle that draws a line showing any changes in blood pressure or pulse. Both of these things, Mr. Doval explains, are affected when someone lies.

"Are you ready, Morgan?" Mr. Doval asks.

"I will be in a moment," she replies. "My ninja training is not just about physical ability. I have learned skills that allow me to control my mind as well."

She brings her hands together in front of her face, closes her eyes, and breathes in and out, in and out.

I feel more relaxed just watching her.

Morgan opens her eyes and nods at Mr. Doval. "I'm ready."

Mr. Doval starts the machine. The paper moves along as the needle draws a perfectly straight line.

"Let's start out with something we know to be true," he says. "What is your name?"

"Morgan."

The needle doesn't waver. The line stays straight.

"Now, please give me a false answer to each of these questions," Mr. Doval says. "How old are you!"

"Seventy-five," Morgan replies.

The needle stays straight.

"Have you ever studied ninja techniques?"

"No."

Again, no change in the needle.

"Okay, one more. How tall are you?"

"Seventeen feet tall," Morgan replies.

I see a small smile start to form along the side of her mouth. I wonder if she's losing control over her ability to fool the machine.

Nope. The needle stays straight as an arrow!

↑

"Thank you, Morgan," says Mr. Doval as he detaches her from the lie detector. "Do you want to share your secrets with the class?"

Morgan shrugs. "I would," she says, "but a good agent never reveals her best tricks." Then she returns to her seat.

Mr. Doval claps.

"Exactly! Thank you, Morgan. A shining example of how to keep information under wraps. Class, please note the first rule of being a spy: Never reveal your secrets!"

As the class ends, I ask Drew, Josh, and Morgan if they would hang around for a few minutes.

"What's up, Billy?" Josh asks after everyone else has left the classroom.

"How well do you guys know my roommate, Xavier?" I ask.

"He's in some of my ninja-training classes," says Morgan. "But I don't know him all that well. He's pretty smart, and his ninja skills are top notch."

"He seems like an okay guy to me," says Josh. "A little weird maybe, but I like him. Why, what's going on?"

"Just a feeling," I admit. I don't want to accuse Xavier of anything, especially since I don't know if he's guilty or not.

"I actually know what you mean, Billy," Drew chimes in. "I can't put my finger on it, but there's something about him that I just don't trust."

"Thanks, Drew. I'm sure it's nothing," I say. But I head off to the invention lab more worried than ever. I like Drew, and I trust him. If he has a bad feeling about Xavier, then maybe I really do have something to be concerned about.

Chapter Ten

Factual, Observational Evidence

BACK AT THE INVENTION LAB I DECIDE TO TAKE a different approach than I have so far. Since I got here, I've been trying to create a full-blown version of Spy Dye, with all its functions working at once. Today, I'll work on creating one aspect of the Spy Dye at a time.

After about two hours, I have a mixture ready to test. One of the features Mom asked me to include in the Spy Dye is the ability to read the thoughts of others, if only for a few seconds. Kind of like Josh!

I fill an eyedropper with a little bit of

the thick black liquid I've come up with and place a single drop onto my hair. I turn my attention to Xavier, who is hard at work a few benches away. I focus my mind on him, straining to concentrate all my attention on his thoughts.

I start to hear a soft voice in my head. It sounds like someone whispering in an echo-filled hallway.

It works! I can hear Xavier's thoughts in my mind. I concentrate even harder, and the thoughts flow from his mind to mine:

Come on, Xavier. You've got to do this. You've got to make this invention perfect. You need to come through for Agent Paul! If only Billy Sure—

And then the voice fades away. The Spy Dye has worn off, and I can no longer hear his thoughts.

What was Xavier thinking about me?!

There is definitely something suspicious about my roommate here at Spy Academy.

I glance back over at Xavier's workstation. Although I'm uncomfortable doing it, I decide

I have to speak with Xavier. He's the only one who could have possibly seen what I was or wasn't doing in the room in the middle of the night.

I walk over to his workstation.

"Hey, roomie," Xavier says. "Want to see something new?" Xavier pops a piece of candy into his mouth. A few seconds later, he's gone. Vanished! No sign of him anywhere!

Then I hear a tiny voice shouting up from the floor. I look down and see that Xavier has shrunk to the size of an action figure. He looks like he could live in a dollhouse!

"Pretty cool, huh?" Xavier squeaks from the floor. "I finally got my MINI CANDY to work."

I see him reach into his (mini) pocket and grab a piece of candy that seems to have shrunk too. He pops it into his mouth and a few seconds later he is full size again—but then he keeps growing and growing until he has to bend over just to keep from hitting his head on the ceiling!

"And my HUMUNGO CANDY works too!"

The candy wears off and Xavier returns to normal size.

"That's amazing," I say, wishing I could be as successful at my invention project. I can just see how Mini Candy and Humungo Candy will help on a rescue mission—just in case our agents need to get past gates or traps.

"So, I wanted to ask you something," I continue. "And it may sound kind of weird. Have you noticed me getting up and working in the middle of the night?"

"You're right," Xavier says, "that does sound

kind of weird. Well, I'm a pretty heavy sleeper, but I never heard or saw you. Why would you do that, anyway? That's just strange."

"Never mind," I say, not having the least desire to explain sleep-inventing to Xavier. "Thanks."

After not making much progress in the lab, I head to dinner, where I meet up with Drew, Josh, and Morgan.

I decide that the time has come to fill them in on what's been happening to me.

"So, I have a real problem," I begin. "I'm worried that someone stole my blueprints."

Drew is quick to respond. "I think Xavier is hiding something," he says. "He always has a secretive look, and today he had dark shadows at approximately one centimeter below his brown eyes. Maybe he stayed up late to steal your blueprints."

"Sounds like factual, observational evidence to me," says Josh. "Like we learned about in class."

"I have to solve this mystery," I say as an idea pops into my head. "And I think I just came up with a plan that might work!"

I don't see Xavier again before I go to bed, and once again, he's gone before I wake up the next morning. But there's good news—after a restless night's sleep, I wake up to a set of blueprints at my desk. They're not Spy Dye blueprints, though. They're blueprints for what I call LIAR'S LEMONADE.

I need to invent a foolproof method to find out whether someone is lying. That's the only way I'm going to get to the bottom of what happened to my Spy Dye blueprints, and after seeing how Morgan fooled the lie detector, I can't trust that device. Instead, I'm going to fine-tune one of the very first ideas I ever had for an invention, back when I was a little kid.

Simply put, Liar's Lemonade is a lemonade drink. When someone drinks it and then lies, his or her face and palms turn bright pink. You can't use mind control or meditation techniques to fool it, because you don't know that it's anything other than a regular glass of lemonade. By the time you tell a lie, it's too late.

At the invention lab, I follow the directions from the blueprints. I start by mixing up a batch of lemonade and adding things like food coloring and sprinkles, plus some top secret—and non-toxic—mind-reading ingredients. Then I mix it over the lie detector. I don't know if that will help, but it can't hurt.

It doesn't take long for me to whip up a completed batch of Liar's Lemonade. If only inventing Spy Dye were this easy, I wouldn't have to go through all of this trouble!

I need to make sure this works, so I test it on myself. I take few sips. **Slurp!** It tastes exactly like regular lemonade, which is important. The

LIAR'S LEMONADE

people I use it on can't have any idea that this lemonade is special.

I look into a mirror and state an obvious lie. "My name is Emily."

After I say the lie, I don't feel any different. But guess what! In the mirror I'm thrilled to see that my face and the palms of my hands have turned bright pink! Perfect! My Liar's Lemonade works like a charm. But oh no. How do I make my skin normal again?

I look into the mirror. Well, if it worked once, maybe it will work the other way?

"My name is Billy Sure."

Blurp blurp blurp! The pink fades away instantly. It's official. My invention works!

Which means now I can get to the bottom of this after all.

I pour a tall glass and head over to Xavier's workstation.

"Hi, Xavier," I say. "I see you're working very hard. I thought you might like a glass of lemonade."

"Thanks, I love lemonade," Xavier replies.

He gulps down the entire glass. "Ah, that was great. Did you make it?"

"Yup," I say proudly.

"So you're a chef as well as an inventor," Xavier says, smiling.

This is just about the friendliest Xavier's ever been. I start to feel kinda bad about fooling him like this, but I have to see if he's behind the blueprint mystery.

"Xavier, do you know what happened to some blueprints that were on my desk the other night?" I ask. It sounds awkward, like it's coming out of left field, which I guess it is.

"I don't know anything about your blueprints," he replies, looking at me like I'm the weirdest kid he's ever met.

I stare at him for a few seconds, searching for any sign that his face or palms are turning pink.

But nope. Nothing. No change at all. Xavier is telling the truth.

Xavier rolls his eyes and shakes his head. "Man, you are one strange kid," he says. "Anyway, thanks for the lemonade."

I walk back to my workbench, thoroughly discouraged. I don't know what my next move should be. I know in my gut that something happened to my blueprints the other night, but I can't prove it.

I'm overwhelmed by the feeling that this whole Spy Academy thing is turning out to be a great big failure. That's when I remember I haven't seen Mom in a few days. She's probably out in the field, looking for Agent Paul, waiting for her son the inventor to offer his help, and here I am with no progress!

Dejected, I head back to my room. Fortunately, as usual, Xavier is working late at the lab, so I can be miserable all by myself. In the hallway I decide to type out a text to Manny, who still hasn't answered any of my messages or e-mails.

> Miss you, partner. I hope you're doing okay, and I hope Emily hasn't annoyed you to death. Let me know how you're doing—I haven't heard from you in a while.

I'll be honest. I'm super worried about why Manny hasn't answered my e-mails. Is he mad at me? Or worse, was he bitten by flying sharks or something?

And then . . . success! As soon as I walk into

the room, there's a **BEEEEP!** It's my cell phone. I have a text message.

It's from Manny!

Billy, I know you are at Spy Academy. We need to talk. Can you do a video chat?

GULP. Um, okay. That was far from the message I was expecting. How can Manny know where I am? Why didn't he let me know? I type back quickly.

Give me one second. Be there ASAP.

I flip open my laptop and connect to Manny for a video chat.

His face pops up on my screen. It's real! He's real! He's Manny! I have never been happier to see anyone.

"What do you mean, you know I'm at Spy Academy? How?" I ask.

"That night before you left, during our sleep-over, you talked in your sleep and told me all about Spy Academy and Spy Dye and everything," Manny explains. "At first I thought it was crazy talk. But not anymore."

I'm stunned.

Manny continues: "And unless I'm mistaken, something weird happened with your blueprints, right?"

Okay, this is beyond crazy. How can Manny possibly know about that?

"Yeah, but how can you . . . I mean . . . what . . . I . . ."

"Let me explain," Manny says calmly. I can use a heaping dose of Manny's calmness right about now. "Ever since you told me about Spy Academy in your sleep, Emily and I have been trying to find out more about it. Also, Emily's new 'thing' is that she paints each of her fingernails a different color."

"I think I noticed that before I left, actually. But I'm confused. Can we get a little closer to the point of this story?" I ask. What does my sister have to do with any of this?

"That's where I'm headed, partner," Manny

replies. "One night Emily and I were looking for information about Spy Academy in your mom's office. Emily picked up what appeared to be a blank piece of paper. She had just finished painting her nails and held her hand up to a lamp to see how the nails looked."

"Why are we still talking about Emily's nails?"

"Hang on. She was still holding the blank piece of paper when she lifted her hand up near the light, only when the light hit the paper, we discovered that it wasn't blank at all. A map appeared on the paper. A map written in Hidden Ink. A map showing the way to Spy Academy!"

Hidden Ink! Xavier's invention!

Manny goes on. "Next, we found a directory of everyone who attends Spy Academy. When we opened it up, it looked like a blank book, but when we held it up to the light too, we saw that the names in the directory were also written with Hidden Ink. Have you looked at yours?"

I realize that honestly, I haven't opened up the directory Mom gave me on my first day at Spy Academy. I dig through a pile of stuff on my desk and find it. Opening the cover, I see that the pages are indeed blank. Then I hold it up to a desk lamp and a list of names appears.

"I never even looked at it," I say.

"Now that you know about the directory, is there someone named Drew at Spy Academy?" Manny asks.

I feel a cold chill run down my spine. Drew?

"Yeah, there is," I say. "We've actually become friends."

"Do you know Drew's last name?" Manny asks.

Huh. Now that Manny mentions it, I guess I never asked Drew what his last name is. All I know is that it begins with an S. I hold the directory up to the light and flip through the pages. I come to Drew's name and gasp.

Swiped! Drew's last name is *Swiped!*

Swiped is the last name of my arch nemesis, Alistair Swiped. Swiped is a so-called inventor who spends more time stealing ideas (mine) and cheating, rather than actually inventing anything himself.

"Could Drew be related to Alistair Swiped? If he's anything like Alistair, he could be the one who stole my blueprints for Spy Dye. Manny, what am I going to do?"

Before Manny can answer, a hooded figure leans into the video chat window and grabs Manny!

And then before I can see anything else, the video goes dead.

"Manny!" I shout at the blank screen on my laptop.

Chapter Eleven

Manny to the Rescue

PANIC FILLS MY ENTIRE BODY AS QUESTIONS RACE through my brain.

Is Manny okay? Who would have possibly grabbed him? And why? And does all this have anything to do with me and Spy Dye? And how am I ever gonna help the Big Rescue Mission, my mom, and Agent Paul?

In the midst of my anxiety, I don't even notice the door to my room opening and someone walking in, until a voice behind me suddenly says:

"Don't worry about Manny."

I spin around and find myself face to face with Drew.

Drew SWIPED!

"What did you do with him?" I ask. Did my best Spy Academy friend just kidnap my real best friend?

"Oh, don't worry," Drew cackles, unable to hold back a smug, self-satisfied smile. "Uncle Alistair will take good care of him."

So that was Alistair? Why? Is Manny all right? And how can the Drew standing in front of me be such a totally different person from the Drew I thought I knew?

"I—I don't understand, Drew," I say. "I thought we were friends."

Drew smiles again, but this time it's a little sad. He stares at me for a moment, then turns and hurries from the room without saying another word. *BAM!* The door slams behind him.

Before I even have time to think, much less to absorb everything that has just happened, I hear a lock being turned in the door to the room—from the outside!

I dash across the room and grab the doorknob.

It won't turn. I yank on it, but it doesn't budge. I think about running to the window, but then I remember that we're underground.

I'm trapped. I'm all alone in the room . . . I'm locked in. I start banging on the door.

Nope. Nothing. Everyone is either in class or working in a lab or in the cafeteria.

I pace the room. My mind is reeling.

Stop! I finally say to myself. Sit down . . . think . . .

Okay, first, Manny and Emily have known all along that I'm at Spy Academy. It makes sense, I guess, that I sleep-talk as well as sleep-invent—and sleep-talk especially when I have crazy spy dreams. So after I let the cat out of the sleeping bag, Emily and Manny figure out that Drew is Alistair Swiped's nephew. Me, I didn't have a clue. I just thought he was my new good buddy.

And then, at exactly the moment these two new startling pieces of information are revealed to me, Alistair Swiped grabs Manny why, I'm not sure.

And then, Drew comes in, changes from nice guy to evil nemesis, and locks me in the room.

Again, why? Why *all* of this?

And, of course, Manny. Is he okay? Where is Alistair taking him? And what do Drew and Alistair want?

This is getting me nowhere. Some spy I am.

Which makes me think. Spy . . . Mom!

I'm so rattled, I missed the obvious. I grab my cell phone and punch in Mom's number.

A message immediately pops up:

All Calls Blocked.

Blocked? This must be some kind of spy training Drew had that I didn't. He must have

somehow stopped my phone from working. I'm totally stuck. I can't leave the room and I can't phone for help.

And what about Manny? With each passing second I get more and more worried about Manny.

Just as I'm thinking this, there's a noise.

CRACK!

It's the sound of the door bursting open!

I jump to my feet in time to see someone stumble into the room, as if he's just been shoved in. But before I can see who did the shoving, the door slams shut and is locked again. The person's hands are tied behind his back and his head is down, but he has a special Sure Things, Inc. button pinned to his shirt.

"Manny!" I cry.

"Nice to see you, partner," he says, lifting his head and forcing a smile.

That's Manny, calm and ready with a joke, even now.

I walk behind him and untie his hands.

"Are you okay?" I ask.

"Yeah, no one hurt me," Manny replies. "Everything just suddenly went dark while I was talking to you. Someone slipped into the office and blindfolded me. Then I was shoved into a car, driven around for a bit, and now I'm here. Whoever did this never said a single word the whole time."

"It was Alistair Swiped," I say. "When I asked about you, Drew said 'Uncle Alistair will take good care of him.' Then he locked me in here. And now you're in here too."

"So, what's been going on at Spy Academy?" Manny asks in his "it's time to get down to business" voice, which at the moment is very comforting to me.

"What *hasn't* been going on at Spy Academy?" I say. I start at the beginning. I explain how I have to invent Spy Dye to save Agent Paul on the Big Rescue Mission, but how I haven't been able to. I talk about my Liar's Lemonade, and of course, the greatest mystery of all: Where are my blueprints for Spy Dye?

When I get to that part, Manny's eyes open

wide. He rubs his chin and scratches his head.

"I don't think your blueprints were blank, Billy," he says, standing up.

"What do you mean?" I ask. "Didn't you hear what I just said?"

"Remember the map I told you about? And the Spy Academy directory? They were both written using Hidden Ink."

"But the pen I used was my own, with normal ink," I explain.

Manny picks up the pen and scribbles on a blank piece of paper. It looks like no ink is coming out of the pen. But when Manny holds the paper up to the lamp, his scribble suddenly appears.

"Someone swapped your regular pen for this one, which is filled with Hidden Ink," Manny says.

And that's when the door to the room swings open and in walks . . . Drew.

Chapter Twelve

Drew Swiped

"OH, BILLY, BILLY, BILLY," DREW SAYS, TAUNTING me by holding up a pen that looks exactly like my pen, because it *is* my pen! "Sorry about the delay in my arrival. I was just discussing matters with Uncle Alistair. He has been telling me all about you and all the problems you've caused for him."

"You mean problems with his business model of stealing my ideas and rushing his junky knockoffs to market before the real inventor can get his out to the public?" I shoot back. "Because we're happy to cause him problems with *that* business anytime," I add.

Drew ignores my little swipe at Swiped. "Usually, I couldn't care less about what Uncle Alistair has to say," Drew continues. "I know about his tendency to 'borrow' the work of others. And as a real inventor myself, I don't have much use for dear old Uncle Alistair. But being a real inventor, this time I do care."

Drew pulls out his phone and streams a video.

"Remember this?" he asks, handing the phone to me. I take it. Manny looks on.

The video shows Drew standing next to a large machine with a flashing light, a huge antenna, and a single seat. He starts to make a presentation about his invention. I don't remember this particular submission (there were many), but I realize instantly that this was one of the entries submitted to our Next Big Thing contest and TV special.

"That's my invention, Billy," Drew says. "A time machine. A time machine that really works! With that caliber of invention, I should have won your little competition, but you rejected me. You were too busy parading around, telling the world that you are the world's best inventor. But here I was, with an actual TIME MACHINE! I'm the best, and nobody even knows it."

I remember this invention now. It's as fake as Drew's friendship with me. Tons of kids submitted ideas for time travel devices. Tons of kids wanted Sure Things, Inc. to make one. But it can't happen. I've learned from years of trying that you just can't mess with the space-time continuum.

I roll my eyes and give Drew back his phone.

"Do you know how many kids try to invent a time machine, Drew?" I say. "We must have seen a dozen submissions just in the Next Big Thing contest alone. It's actually *the* most popular invention idea. But so far, no one has come up with one that works. My guess is that no one ever will."

"You see, that's where you're wrong, Billy," Drew says. "Mine does work, but you didn't even give me a chance! It works, and I can prove it!"

DREW SWIPED

INVENTOR OF THE FIRST
FLYING HOVERCRAFT

Drew reaches into his pocket and pulls out a page that he has torn from a magazine. Manny unfolds it, and I see that it's an advertisement for a flying hovercraft.

I gasp. I can't believe it. The ad shows Drew

standing next to a hovercraft which looks exactly like the design for a hovercraft that Manny and I have been working on for the past few months. We haven't quite perfected it, but it appears that somehow Drew has.

The caption under the photo reads: *Drew Swiped, inventor of the first flying hovercraft.*

"How did you invent the hovercraft?" I ask. "And how could we not know about it? And how can yours look exactly like the one Manny and I have been working on?"

"You did do a good job of keeping your hovercraft design a secret," Drew says. "But, you see, I have a working time machine. I went into the future to the day you completed your hovercraft, stole the design, and came back so I could beat you to it."

Like uncle, like nephew, I think.

"And get a load of this," Drew says, pulling something out of his back pocket.

It's a blueprint! A blueprint for Spy Dye! Only this one is plainly visible—and in Drew's handwriting.

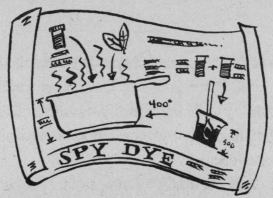

"Not only did I sneak into your room and switch pens, but the next day I came back and stole the Spy Dye blueprints. You were supposed to have no idea you invented it, so you wouldn't even look for them," Drew explains.

"But what you didn't count on was the fact that I knew I wrote out the blueprints because my pen was moved," I add.

But I also don't know what to think. It seems to me that Drew has pulled off the perfect crime. I have no way of proving that I invented Spy Dye first.

But the best is yet to come.

"And last, but not least, is this," Drew says.

He holds out a contract. "This is a deal I made with Savino Airlines to mass produce my hovercraft," he boasts. "Here."

I take the contract from Drew, and Manny and I look it over. I see that it is signed by Drew and by John Savino, president of Savino Airlines. It calls for the mass production of Drew's hovercraft.

"Look at the date," Drew says.

The date of the contract is six months from now!

"So you see, my time machine really does work," Drew says. "I went into the future, took your hovercraft idea, and made this deal. And, I'll do it again. So you have two choices. You can either keep on creating inventions, and I'll just jump into the future, steal them, then come back and release them before you do. Or you can stop inventing altogether.

"Either way, Billy Sure, your career is finished. Say hello to Drew Swiped, the next kid entrepreneur!"

I'm finished. Done. My career over at the ripe old age of thirteen. I see no way out of this one.

That's when Manny takes over.

"I disagree, Drew," he says calmly. "By the

way, I'm Manny. I don't believe we've been properly introduced." How can Manny be so polite at a time like this?!

"What I do believe, however, is that we are firmly planted in the present, where I have been recording this entire conversation on my phone. Good catch blocking calls, by the way. Thankfully, other apps still work. So now I have an audio recording of you admitting to stealing the hovercraft idea and Billy's design for Spy Dye," Manny continues.

"So, unless you want me to go straight to the head of Spy Academy and hand the recording over, you'll give us the blueprints for Spy Dye. And, oh yeah, we know your time machine is a fake. Don't we, Billy?"

I'm too stunned by Manny's speech to say anything at first. He seems to have instantly turned the tables on Drew just when I thought we were finished.

I finally manage to say, "That's right!"

Drew's eyes narrow. "What do you mean 'time machine is a fake'?" he says. "I know about the hovercraft. I have a signed contract—from the future!"

"Really?" Manny says, pretending to be surprised. "Well then, why don't we drink a toast to your time machine?"

Manny turns to me. "Billy, do you have any of your delicious lemonade around?"

This is where I'm really glad that Drew locked me in my dorm room with its mini fridge and not someplace more random.

I grab a pitcher of Liar's Lemonade and pour three glasses, handing one to each of us.

"To Drew's time machine," Manny says, raising his glass.

Drew is hesitant, but the lemonade smells really good, and I see him take a sip.

"So tell me, Drew, did you really invent a time machine that really works?" Manny asks immediately.

"Yes!" Drew insists.

What do you know? His face and hands turn bright pink!

Aha!

"That was some of my Liar's Lemonade," I admit, as Drew stares in horror at his colorful hands. "And you, my friend, are a liar!"

I turn to Manny. "How did you know?"

Manny shrugs, as if this amazing feat of spy work he just pulled off is no big deal.

"I figured that the hovercraft ad was fake," he begins. "It's easy enough to doctor a photo. But I must admit that the Savino Airlines contract is pretty impressive."

Manny holds up the contract and looks at Drew. "And you even got your hands on some Savino Airlines letterhead. Very nice touch. However, you didn't do your homework, Drew.

"I read four business publications every day, which is how I know that John Savino, the founder of Savino Airlines, turned the company over to his daughter, Joan, about a month ago.

"So, if you really had gone six months into the future and signed a contract with Savino Airlines, Joan Savino would have signed it, since she is now the president of the company. This signature says: John Savino. It's a fake. And so are you!"

Drew's head drops. His plan has been exposed and defeated. He hands over the blueprints for Spy Dye.

"Stupid Savino Airlines," he mutters.

"So it turns out that Manny is the best spy of all!" I say. "And he didn't even have to go to the academy!"

"So the question now is, what do we do with Drew," Manny says.

"It's tempting to report Drew to the academy," I say. "After all, you have recorded evidence. But Drew *is* good at spying. He must have spied in my notebook to find out what we want the hovercraft to look like. And if he stays here, he'll be spying for the agency and not on Sure Things, Inc.!"

I wonder what kind of mental image Drew's forming of me—Billy Sure, thirteen years old, blond hair, *not* a spy.

"I will, however, have to tell my mom about

all this," I tell him. "She should be keeping a closer eye on you."

My mom!

It suddenly hits me that I now have a working blueprint for Spy Dye. Only Drew is blocking the door. How will we get out?

At that moment there's a rustling at the door. Oh no. Alistair Swiped is probably coming inside! What if he takes Manny's cell phone with the recording?

The dorm door swings open. But it's not Alistair Swiped that walks in. It's XAVIER!

Xavier looks at Drew. Drew backs away from the door. Xavier glares at Manny. He eyes the rope on the floor that was tied around Manny's hands. He stares at me.

"Billy Sure, you're one strange kid," Xavier says, shaking his head.

"Xavier!" I yelp. "You're here!"

Xavier's brow furrows.

"Yeah," he says. "I live here too."

Who knew Xavier, my roommate, would be saving me from Drew, my former friend?

"I've got to take these blueprints to the lab and whip up a batch of Spy Dye," I say. "Manny, can you find my mom? And make sure Drew doesn't get into any more mischief!"

"Absolutely," Manny says. "Drew, you're going to do as *we* say. Xavier is a witness now too. Come with me!"

Xavier looks at Manny like he has no clue who he is, but shrugs. "As long as we're not getting any more roommates," he says, probably wondering why Manny is here in the first place.

Drew reluctantly follows Manny out the door.

Meanwhile, I scurry to the lab, where, thanks to my blueprints, it doesn't take long to whip up a working batch of Spy Dye. I test it, and sure enough it allows me to read minds, hide devices, and project a personal force field. It also records conversations—which Mom didn't request, but I figured might come in handy.

A short while later, Manny shows up at the lab with Mom.

"Here's the Spy Dye, just like you ordered, Mom," I say, handing a big batch of the inky liquid over to her. "Manny told you about Drew, right?"

"Oh yes, we'll be keeping an eye on him," says Mom. "And thanks, Billy. This is great work. I am sure we'll have Agent Paul back in no time."

I smile. I wish I could have spent more time with Mom, but at least I accomplished what she brought me here to do.

After giving Manny a tour of the complex, Mom, Manny, and I head to the cafeteria for dinner. Manny gets a kick out of the vanishing vanilla ice cream. Then Mom stands up from the staff table.

Ding! Ding! Ding! She taps on her glass three times.

"Excuse me, students," Mom announces. "By now, you've likely heard that one of our best agents was caught by enemy spies. We have employed over one hundred agents for a rescue mission, aptly named the Big Rescue Mission.

"Tonight, I am happy to report that Agent Paul was brought home safely, thanks to the inventions of our lovely inventors. Everyone, please give a round of applause for Sylvia, with her Palm Power 5000; Xavier, with his Mini Candy and Humungo Candy; and Billy, with his Spy Dye!"

There's a burst of applause. Manny makes me stand up. I really don't like being in the spotlight, but it feels good knowing that everyone is safer now because of my invention!

After eating my last bite of flaming flan (my favorite), Mom swings by my seat.

"So, how was your time here?" she asks me. "Do you think maybe you'd like to stay here and

be a student at SPY ACADEMY full-time?"

Mom's offer is tempting. And, before my adventure here, it was exactly what I wanted. But you know what else? I miss my regular life: my schoolwork, my time with Philo, even Emily. Mostly, though, I miss working with Manny every day—Manny, who was the best spy all along!

"Thanks, Mom, but I think I'd like to go back home," I say.

Mom nods. I can see she's disappointed, but she understands, too. My home is back at our house, Manny's garage, and Fillmore Middle School.

The next day Manny and I get into the same unmarked car Mom brought me in to go home.

"You know, Manny, since no one has really invented a time machine yet, the future is still a mystery," I say. "But one thing that's not a mystery is that I think the time has come for us to perfect a hovercraft."

"It's the Next Big Thing, for sure!" Manny

replies. Then he looks around the car. "But, Billy, why is there an octopus in this car?"

I look over at the tank.

"Oh, that's Paul," I say, smiling. "My mom is really glad to have her partner back. And so am I."

I'm Billy Sure—pizza lover, dog owner, and young inventor. I do a lot of different things, including talking to my mom over video chat. Why do I talk to her over video chat? Because my mom has a super-confidential, top-secret secret—she's a spy, and she's always off doing spy things!

Yup, that's right, my mom is a spy, complete with coded messages, hidden documents, secret missions . . . you know, all the cool spy stuff.

So sometimes, when she's away on secret missions, the only way I can talk to her is over video chat. Like now.

"I miss you, Billy," Mom says from my laptop screen. "I can't believe it's been two weeks!"

"Me too," I say. "Wow. Two weeks already!"

Okay, so backstory. I didn't always know my mom is a spy. In fact, I only just found out a few weeks ago. Mom used to claim she was a scientist doing research for the government. I thought this was true until my thirteenth birthday, when she surprised me by sharing her real profession. And then she surprised me even more by taking me to her agency's Spy Academy, where I took spy classes and built an invention to save secret agents on dangerous missions.

This is all 100 percent real. Mom asked me to help her because she was so impressed with all the inventions my company, Sure Things, Inc., has produced. Our inventions include the All Ball, which turns into any sports ball; the Sibling Silencer, which, uh, silences your siblings; and the Stink Spectacular, which smells super gross but tastes super great. We're also the company that created Gross-to-Good Powder, which makes gross food taste delicious. (If you eat in my school cafeteria, you're welcome!) Our latest invention is the No-Trouble Bubble, an impenetrable bubble where nothing can get to you. (Not even those silenced siblings!)

But it's been a while since Sure Things, Inc. has come out with a new product, what with my being away inventing at Spy Academy. That was a lot of fun, but I realized that I'm not cut out to be a full-fledged secret agent. I also missed my best friend and Sure Things, Inc.'s CFO, Manny Reyes. So I decided to come home, even if it meant going back to boring "normal" school and dealing with Emily, my boring "normal" older sister.

Like Mom said, it's been two weeks since I got home from Spy Academy, and this video chat is the first time I get to catch up with her. Seeing her face is really nice. I can almost forget that she isn't safe and sound at home, rather than fighting dangerous katana-wielding Ninjas in—well, who knows where the lair of dangerous katana-wielding Ninjas is!

"It feels like I was just at Spy Academy," I tell Mom, "although I've been pretty busy. That's because I told everyone I was on vacation in Barbados, and I had to do a whole report on my trip in social studies class. Thankfully, Manny helped me with that research."

Mom laughs.

"Sorry about the extra assignment. Has the rest of school been all right?" she asks.

"It's been okay. When I was away, the Fillmore Middle School Inventors Club elected a temporary president. Do you remember Clayton Harris?"

"Of course!" Mom says. "He was, um—"

"Not super cool, yeah," I say. "His favorite activity is going to the dentist. Well, he was elected club president, and I decided to let him keep that position. I still want to help the club, but I don't have time to run the day-to-day details anymore. Besides, Clayton has done really well as the president. He's found his place. He's made new friends, he's a good leader of the club, and he's even become kind of popular—or at least less unpopular."

Mom smiles widely. "That is wonderful!" she says. "Who knows, maybe Clayton will be President of the country someday, all thanks to your club!"

I try to imagine Clayton running for

President or nestled into Mount Rushmore or kissing babies, but all I can picture is the same kid who blew chocolate milk out of his nose at my birthday party.

"And how are things at Sure Things, Inc.? Is Emily still helping out?" Mom asks.

"Sure Things, Inc. is okay," I say. "Manny and I are working on something really big—a hovercraft. And now we're feeling the pressure to get this invention out as our Next Big Thing." Just to fill you in, our hovercraft is going to be the coolest invention ever. It'll really fly and it'll change the face of transportation as we know it. There's just one little problem. We haven't quite figured out how to make it fly. Manny is waiting on some "quality winged materials" to arrive from overseas. I'm not sure exactly what that means, but Manny says they're the latest in hover technology.

"As for Emily, she and Manny got along okay while I was away, but she's been in a pretty grumpy mood ever since I got home."

"What now?" asks Mom. "I talked to her on her birthday a few days ago and she seemed perfectly happy."

Right—Emily's fifteenth birthday. She might have been all smiles on her video chat with Mom, but the day was anything but fun for me and Dad.

It began like this: Emily woke up and started whining for Dad to take her to get her learner permit. Honestly, I didn't see why the permit was such a big deal. All it does is allow her to take a driver's test next year when she's sixteen—or to drive with an instructor now. It's not like she can pick up her friends and go to the mall.

But anyway, Emily kept complaining.

Dad tried to remind her that it was a weekend, so the drivers office was closed.

"It's not fair," she sniffed. "Mom took Billy on a trip for his birthday! No one's offered me a trip. I want to go somewhere. And I can't even get my stupid driver's permit."

"Actually, I was working the whole time I

was at Spy Academy," I tried to remind her, but Emily ignored me. Emily usually ignores things I say when they don't support her argument. So she complained all day until the next morning when Dad took her to the driver's office first thing. Then Emily started pestering Dad about when he would take her out to learn to drive.

I tell Mom all of this and watch her expression change to a frown.

"I wish I could be there to teach her how to drive," she says. "I always feel so guilty that work keeps me away from you kids."

"It's okay," I tell her. "Dad will totally teach Emily how to drive, but he's just a little busy right now. His artwork was accepted to an art gallery."

My dad is an artist, and a pretty good one—if you consider close-ups of my dog Philo's toenails "pretty good." He has a studio in the backyard—a converted garden shed, actually, but he likes it. He can spend days at a time out there painting and be perfectly happy. I'll never understand why a gallery is interested in his wacky portraits, but I'm proud of him anyway.

Mom must be thinking the same thing I am because she starts to laugh, which makes me laugh. In a few seconds we're both roaring to the point of tears, imagining Dad at an art gallery showing fancy art-lovers some portraits of Philo's butt!

"So what's going on over at Spy Academy?" I ask when I stop laughing long enough to catch my breath. "How's Agent Paul?"

Agent Paul is my mom's partner on her spy missions. And oh yeah, he just happens to be an octopus.

"He's doing swimmingly," Mom replies, chuckling at her own silly joke, one I'm sure she's made a hundred times before.

"But seriously," she continues, "I've been keeping a very close eye on Drew. So far, at least, he seems to be behaving. He even helped us catch another online scam artist."

I frown at the mention of Drew. At Spy

Academy I became very close friends with him, but then Manny found out my new friend is actually the nephew of Sure Things, Inc.'s arch nemesis, Alistair Swiped, CEO of Swiped Stuff, Inc. That wouldn't have been a problem, except Drew was trying to sabotage my inventions the whole time! Like uncle, like nephew, I guess. I let Mom know, but she thought it was best for Drew to stay at Spy Academy. Maybe some of his evil genius can be tamed under careful supervision.

Now that I stop to think about it, it really is amazing how much has gone on in the couple of weeks since I got back. Just talking about all of it makes me tired . . . which reminds me that I've got a busy day of school and inventing ahead tomorrow.

"I think I'm going to go to sleep, Mom," I say. "Lots to do tomorrow. We've really got to get this hovercraft out ASAP."

"Okay, honey, get some sleep. I love you."

"I love you too, Mom," I say.

My monitor goes blank.

I'm always a little sad at the end of a video chat with Mom, but somehow, knowing the truth about her makes it all a bit easier. My mom is off saving people. And that's pretty cool.

The next morning I slide into my chair at the breakfast table. Emily is already sitting at the table, sulking, her face buried in her phone. Dad stands at the griddle, flipping something round, red, and gooey. (No way can those gooey things be pancakes.)

"It's a pancake morning," Dad announces, sliding a stack off the griddle and onto a big platter. I guess I was wrong. "Tomato pancakes to be exact."

Emily groans but doesn't say anything. My dad isn't exactly a world-class chef, but he thinks he is. He's always coming up with crazy meals and making us force them down. He's actually more like a mad scientist of food, and his dishes are his monsters!

I do eat tomatoes in omelets sometime, so maybe tomatoes in pancakes won't be too bad. Still, I glance over at the Gross-to-Good Powder in the salt shaker on the table, glad that it's always there.

"Pancakes, not waffles, huh?" I say to Dad. "I guess this means that Mom isn't coming home anytime soon."

One of the many things I learned during my time at Spy Academy was that some of Dad's crazy food concoctions are actually secret coded messages from my mom. Because she's a spy, her e-mails are always in danger of being hacked, so she and Dad worked out a system. For example, waffles mean that Mom will be coming home soon, and different ingredients in the waffles stand for other information. Dad doesn't have to make the dishes, but he usually does anyway. Tomato pancakes mean . . . well, I'm not exactly sure what tomato pancakes mean.

"Nope, your mother is off on assignment," Dad says, confirming what I thought. "I picked pancakes to make, specifically tomato pancakes, because I thought they'd make an excellent subject for my next painting."

"Of course Mom's not coming home," Emily chimes in, finally taking her eyes off of her phone. "Why should she come home? After all, if my fifteenth birthday wasn't important enough to come home for, why should she come home now?"

I want to remind Emily that she and Mom video-chatted on her birthday, but I think better of it. We're probably going to have to hear about how Mom didn't come home for Emily's fifteenth birthday all the way up until she turns sixteen. And worse, she's just getting started.

"Not only didn't I get a visit, but I'm not getting a birthday beach trip," Emily continues as Dad places a stack of tomato pancakes on the table.

I consider bringing up the point once again that I didn't exactly get a birthday beach vacation either. And that my "vacation" was working, going to school, and foiling a dastardly plot by an evil genius. But if there's anything

I know about my older sister, it's that talking to her when she's grumpy leads to bad news. I shove a pancake into my mouth and pretend to concentrate really hard on chewing.

Glug! Uh-oh. I should not have crammed the entire pancake into my mouth. Now it's too late to sprinkle Gross-to-Good Powder on it, and let's just say: tomato pancakes? Not delicious.